VIRTUAL DESTINY

R. J. REIBER

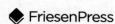 FriesenPress

One Printers Way
Altona, MB R0G 0B0
Canada

www.friesenpress.com

Copyright © 2023 by R. J. Reiber
First Edition — 2023

All rights reserved.

No part of this publication may be reproduced in any form, or by any means, electronic or mechanical, including photocopying, recording, or any information browsing, storage, or retrieval system, without permission in writing from FriesenPress.

ISBN
978-1-03-914297-8 (Hardcover)
978-1-03-914296-1 (Paperback)
978-1-03-914298-5 (eBook)

Fiction, Science Fiction, Time Travel

Distributed to the trade by The Ingram Book Company

PROLOGUE

My name is Kaylee Parker. I was born to my loving parents, Don and Sara, on May 18, 2035. I was diagnosed at birth with a rare incurable spinal cord defect, which means I have no feeling in my legs or feet. My parents were told I would never be able to walk and that I would need a high level of care, making me a "special needs" child.

During my infancy, I was amenable to all the attention and care that I received. That changed when I reached the age of four. My mother would take me to the park in my wheelchair, and I would see other kids running and playing. On one occasion, I became outraged at being captive in the wheelchair and had a severe temper tantrum. I even tried to get out of my wheelchair and fell forward onto the sidewalk. After that, we didn't go to the park very often.

I first met my best friend, Jess, when we were in grade four. We bonded instantly. Jess is an African American and the same age as me. She has a bubbly, fun-loving personality, but she is not overly daring or adventurous. I liked her curly black hair and her amazing smile. She made me laugh.

As I grew older, I became more rebellious. When I was in grade five, a boy with a scooter challenged me to a race. We went to the top of a downhill grade at the end of our street. At the bottom of the hill was a T-intersection with a three-way stop where our street ended. Jess warned me not to do it, but as usual, I didn't listen. The boy and I both left the starting line at the same time and picked up speed quickly. It was exhilarating, and I felt the adrenaline kicking in. He had a lot more control over his scooter than I did in my wheelchair, and then I suddenly realized I had no brakes or steering. Not only that, a car was approaching the intersection from our left, slowing for the stop sign just as we ran the stop sign at the end of our street, crossing the intersection at maximum speed. At that moment, I think we both learned the true meaning of the word "panic." We both overran the low-profile curb and then collided with a hedge that ran perpendicular to our direction of travel along the adjacent sidewalk. The motorist at the intersection hurried over to see if we were OK and then called our parents. We were both a bit scraped up from the hedge but otherwise fine. When my parents found out what happened, they grounded me for two weeks.

When I was in grade ten, a boy offered me a ride on his motorcycle, and I jumped at the opportunity to be free of my wheelchair. As we rode around on local streets, I had never felt so euphoric. However, one of our neighbours ratted me out, and I was grounded once again.

Being trapped in a wheelchair, I went through bouts of depression and extreme anger. Sometimes I wished I could just die, and other times I wanted to lash out at the other kids playing in the park. I was determined that one day I would be able to run and play too.

At a young age, I also began to notice that everyone treated me in a sympathetic manner, almost as if they were expressing their condolences for my being captive in a wheelchair. Why could they not treat me like everyone else?

My parents were grateful that I was an A+ student throughout my school years, from grade one to twelve, except for physical education classes, from which I was exempt. There were no PE programs for people with disabilities, so I would use that time to work on homework assignments in the library. I would also dream of one day finding a cure for my condition so I could run and play and be just like all the other kids.

The following story explains how my childhood dream eventually came true. Little did I realize how it would shape not only my destiny, but also that of the entire planet—changing my life and the fate of humankind forever.

CHAPTER 1

It's 6:30 a.m. as I navigate the narrow, dimly lit hallway as it winds past many offices. As I approach the Research Institute lab's entrance, I hold my security wristband close to the scanner next to the door. The door release activates, and I struggle, as usual, to gain entry into the lab as my wheelchair catches on the doorframe while the lab door tries to close.

"Damn wheelchair," I mutter.

The lab lighting turns on automatically as I reach my cubicle and power up my terminal. I'm always the first person to arrive at the lab so I can work on my own personal research before the other personnel arrive.

Officially, we're working on the human DNA structure and the dynamics of the human brain. Personally, I am secretly working on a process to fix my spinal cord so I can walk. Some of the work we're currently doing pertains to tissue regrowth, but the pace of advancement is too slow for my liking. My accelerated program of tissue-regrowth research is far more advanced and looks promising to eventually fix my spinal cord.

I hear the lab door open and quickly close my research file as the first of three lab technicians arrives.

"Good morning, Kaylee," Tara says cheerfully.

"Good morning. Happy Wednesday," I reply.

Tara started at the Research Institute the same day as I did, and she has a passion for research and applies herself well.

Just then the lab door opens again, and Logan swings by my cubicle.

"Mornin', Kaylee."

"Mornin' to you, Logan."

Logan is intelligent and an adventurer. He is tall and lanky and enjoys almost any outdoor activity if it challenges him sufficiently.

Last, as usual, but not least, Katrina arrives and moves quickly to her cubicle without speaking to anyone. My lab team works well together, despite Katrina not being much of a people person.

"OK, everyone," I say. "It's time for our daily status meeting."

Everyone approaches my cubicle, with Katrina being the last to arrive.

I turn to Tara. "How's the DNA mapping of the human hand going?"

"Coming along slowly. I wish there was a way to speed up the process."

I have to bite my lip as I have secretly developed a method to complete DNA mapping one hundred times faster than the current process is capable of doing.

"Logan, how about you?" I ask.

"I'm organizing the sea slug tissue-regrowth experiment as we speak and should have it ready by the end of today."

"That's great. Let me know if you run into any roadblocks. Katrina, how's the human-brain data movement study coming along?"

"There are some unexplained thought-transmission elements emerging that will require further analysis," Katrina replies. "The main data-movement corridors are being determined, and there are many to evaluate."

"Do you think your assessment will be completed on time? Do you need additional resources to move things along?"

Katrina shakes her head. "I don't need any help. The assessment will be done by the due date."

"OK," I reply, nodding. "Let's get to it."

Logan smiles as he and Tara chat briefly before heading off to start their day. Logan has a crush on Tara, but she does not feel likewise.

Following a busy morning, I spot Tara and Logan sitting at our usual table in the cafeteria, already midway through their meal. I roll up next to Logan and unpack my lunch.

"Logan, did you go mountain biking last night?" I ask.

"I did, and I have some scrapes and cuts on my legs to prove it."

"Did you have to go to the clinic?" Tara asks.

"No, not like the last time when I collided with a tree."

"I would give anything just to ride a mountain bike and take the same risks as you," I say. "Someday."

Later in the afternoon, Logan approaches my cubicle.

"Hi, Kaylee. The brine tanks are set up and populated with sea slugs, so you can start the experiment anytime you like.

Oh, the video camera, pico-probes, and surgical tools are ready as well."

"OK. Thanks, Logan."

While reviewing archived tissue-regrowth material, I came across a fascinating study that was completed twenty-four years ago. Fortunately, many preserved specimens were made available from the California State University, Los Angeles campus, and among them is a quantity of cryogenically frozen sea slugs. I studied the documentation and learned that they can regrow an exact copy of their entire body, including the heart. I also learned that scientists believe the reason the sea slugs detach and regrow their bodies is to replace their parasite-afflicted bodies that degrade their health and sexual performance.

After everyone leaves for the day, I rest my arms on the table next to the brine tanks and rest my chin on my arms. I watch the sea slugs as they move slowly about in the brine tanks and wonder how such a simple creature can possess the incredible ability to replicate almost all of its body.

"You're going to share your tissue-regrowth secrets with me, aren't you?" I whisper. "I'm sure you want to help me fix my spinal cord."

I plan some experiments that are approved by management. They include sea slug memory mapping and the brain's electro-chemical responses related to the regrowth of their bodies The experiments will employ a new technology where tiny wireless intelligent pico-probes are injected into the sea slugs, allowing the contents of their memory to be captured and then analyzed. The purpose of the experiments is to try to understand how sea slugs can reproduce their bodies. Another experiment involves studying the bioelectric code that directs the genes and proteins to regrow an exact copy of the sea slug's body. Many questions need to be answered, and I am determined to answer all of them.

First, I plan to chronicle the regrowth of a sea slug's body by capturing highly magnified images of the progression from start to finish. We'll witness the biogenetic building blocks necessary for the sea slug to recreate its body over a twenty-day period. After studying the regrowth images, my lab techs and I agree that the sea slug's ability to regrow its body is one of nature's finest achievements.

Next, intelligent pico-probes are injected into three sea slugs while their bodies are fully intact and living a normal life. The pico-probes seek out memory data from the sea slugs' brains and transmit the contents to an external data-collection hub connected to a central host computer. A large amount of data is captured but not enough to detail the composition of each and every molecule contained in the sea slug's body. I study the data day and night to try to put the pieces together. My assistants work extra hours as well to better understand what is happening as the sea slugs' bodies regrow.

To understand how the sea slug orchestrates the regrowth process, a bioelectric code analysis is required. For this exercise, intelligent pico-probes are injected and dispersed across the zone where the sea slug's body has been severed from the head. As the sea slug's body regrows, a series of bioelectric impulses seem to direct the process. Even more amazing is that the new growth is protein driven and genetically directed by the layer of tissues that have just been created. I study the results of this experiment extensively and try to understand how the sea slug's memory data is conveyed to the regrowth site.

At this point, I am growing frustrated that we haven't solved all of the mysteries surrounding the tissue-regrowth process. We carry out more experiments on various creatures, including salamanders that regrow their tails. My team and I continue our analysis of the regrowth data for one full year. We're stumped and can't figure out how the regrowth process works until one night when I am nearly asleep at my desk. Suddenly, I realize that the sea slug's brain doesn't arbitrarily send the information. The tissue reconstruction site pulls the DNA data as needed from various sources and uses it to stimulate the regrowth process in a self-managed manner. I immediately text my lab techs and tell them that I think I've figured out the tissue-regrowth process, telling them we can discuss it in the morning.

I am so excited that I don't think I'll be able to sleep.

I text Jess.

"I did it! I did it! I figured it out!"

"Hey. You do realize that it's 3:30 a.m., when most mortals are asleep, right? What did you do that's so important?"

Jess is my one and only lifelong friend. We have known each other since grade four.

"I figured out how the tissue-regrowth process works, so now I can fix my spinal cord!"

"That's fantastic! I know that you and your team have worked so hard, and I hope that one day you and I can go for a walk on the promenade."

"Come and join me at our favourite café after I finish work tomorrow."

"OK. See you there."

After a busy day, I keep a careful eye on the clock as 5:00 p.m. approaches. I don't want to be late leaving work to meet with Jess.

When I arrive, she is seated at our usual table.

"Hey, how is our government workaholic doing today?" Jess asks.

"Well, if you must know, I'm super excited about my tissue-regrowth research. And you?"

"My workday, if you want to call it that, was very leisurely since I refuse to have anything to do with the government running my life."

"Why are you so adamant about the government not controlling your life?"

"I'll tell you why," Jess states. "When I was in grade two, a well-meaning white town councillor believed that in order to promote racial integration amongst the younger population, we should be bused across town to attend the public school there and intermingle with the white kids.

"The classrooms were organized to have the white kids on one side and us on the other. Class discipline was very strict. If my teacher thought you were misbehaving, she would slap you repeatedly with a ruler on the palm of your hand. I was slapped a few times and I don't know what I did to provoke her. It seemed to me that the coloured kids were slapped a lot more than the white kids.

"Out in the playground, the white kids would either ignore us or taunt us with racial slurs. Some of us were physically abused by being punched or kicked.

"Busing us across town only lasted for one school year after our parents complained bitterly of how we were being treated by both the teachers and the white kids.

"I hated every minute of that school year and, from that day onward, despised any form of government control of my life. There. That's my rant on government control."

"That's terrible. I can't imagine what it must have been like to have to endure such abuse," I say with empathy. "Now I get where you're coming from."

"The only thing I want to do is get out of Los Angeles and be free," Jess replies. "I'm thinking of joining a commune on the outskirts of LA where everyone lives a free lifestyle. You can come with me if you want."

"You know I can't do that. I have to fix my spinal cord before considering other lifestyle options."

"I get it. So, tell me about your tissue-regrowth discovery. You seemed pretty excited last night."

"It's so simple, but I couldn't see it. I finally figured out that if intelligent nano-probes are deposited at my damaged spinal cord location, they can direct the tissue-regrowth activity and fuel the repair process to fix my spinal cord."

"Are you sure it will work?" Jess asks. "Aren't you taking a huge risk? What if something goes wrong?"

"Yes, the process requires further testing before I try it on myself."

"When you're ready to experiment on yourself, you better tell me so I can call for help if I need to."

"OK," I reply with a nod. "I guess that makes sense."

CHAPTER 2

After completing the tedious exercise of identifying each and every spinal cord nerve connection, I spend the next three weeks developing a code sequence to restore the nerve terminations that will enable me to walk. I'm so excited about the prospect of walking that I ignore the uncertainty factor of the experiment not being successful and plan to covertly perform the procedure the following night.

The wait is over. Late at night, I hold my wristband up to the scanner and enter the Research Institute's side entrance that offers admittance to the various research labs. I'm the only person there, as I had hoped. Upon entry to my lab, the overhead lights automatically activate. As I am approaching my desk, Wade Siskin, the night security guard, pops his head in to say hello.

"I saw you entering on the security monitor," he says. "Working late again?"

Somewhat startled, I turn to face him. "Yeah. I like the peace and quiet so I can work with no distractions."

Wade nods. "Makes sense. Just checking to make sure everything is OK. Call me if you need anything."

"OK, thanks. I will."

Once Wade leaves, I can begin my experiment. After doing my own tissue-regrowth research well into the night, I have checked and rechecked my data files and am about to perform an unauthorized procedure to hopefully improve my mobility, if all goes well. I anxiously re-examine my data file to check one last time that my calculations and data entries are correct, knowing there is no room for error.

"Hey, Jess, I'm about to run the tissue-regrowth procedure. Wish me luck."

A minute later, Jess responds, not at all enthused with me experimenting on myself.

"Are you sure you want to do this? How long will it take? Tell me when it's over so I know you're OK."

"It should take about an hour and a half. I'll call you."

The outcome of the procedure can go one of two ways: either I'll have improved feeling and mobility in my legs, or my nervous system could be adversely affected with unwelcome side effects, such as pain or paralysis afflicting other parts of my body. The research up to now has been theoretically promising but is untried on a human subject. I save and exit my program and then head over to the test chamber. I download my program into the control module of the laser-powered guidance system used to direct the movement of a robotic arm mounted on a rolling cart next to the operating table. Intelligent nano probes suspended in a saline solution are fed into a syringe mounted on the robotic arm. Next, I remove my pants and top and lower my underwear to expose my lower back. I use an alcohol swab to cleanse the location where the syringe will penetrate my spine.

The operating table's overhead lamps activate while I struggle to pull myself up onto the operating table and make myself comfortable while lying on my stomach. The control module is positioned within easy reach to allow me to initiate the procedure. After positioning a temporary prototype uplink port behind my right ear, which is held in place with an elasticized strap to secure it on my neck, I put on a clear plastic mask and then attach a communication cable, originating at the control module. It clips onto my temporary uplink port, which is a prototype computer interface to my brain with a special connector that locks in place. Everything is ready to begin the procedure, so, without delay, I press the green "start" button on the control module.

The operating table lighting turns off, and I receive just enough sleeping gas, also known as "happy gas," to put me into a deep sleep to ensure I remain motionless. After a few seconds, the control module directs the robotic arm to position itself directly over my lower spine. Laser light from a laser projection head at the end of the robotic arm illuminates my lower back with the image of a small red target.

After a few precision adjustments are completed to position the target accurately, an elongated syringe penetrates my spine and injects intelligent nano-probes into the spinal cord defect region. They will send and receive brain impulses to facilitate the tissue-regrowth process. The syringe retracts to the standby position, and a nearby video monitor shows a cross section of my spinal cord. On an adjacent display, a spinal-cord wiring diagram appears, showing hundreds of terminations, with many in red and a few in blue. Blue is good, and red is bad, signifying open or incomplete terminations. I have made a list of terminations that need to be completed based upon previous analytical test procedures. Data is fed to my brain via my uplink port that will stimulate new tissues to grow and connect individual nerve endings one at a time to restore functionality to my lower appendages. The nano probes at the regrowth site will direct and monitor all restoration activity throughout the procedure as it continues with many terminations to repair.

Without warning, the incoming electrical service to the Research Institute is interrupted for a few seconds, and the procedure stops. When I awaken, the control module has terminated the procedure, and the robotic arm has retracted as the operating table lights turn on. I have great expectations, thinking my spinal cord is fixed, only to find out that the monitor has rebooted and is displaying a "Procedure Aborted—Invalid Data" message. I have some limited feeling in my legs but not enough to walk.

I feel very dejected as I remove the uplink port, harness, and face mask and manoeuvre myself back into my wheelchair. As I remove the temporary uplink port, the left side of my face is in agony, feeling as if my facial muscles have tensed and won't relax. While getting dressed, I notice that my left arm and left leg are hurting in a similar manner.

Returning to my desk, feeling frustrated, I notice that I need to reboot my terminal. Upon review of the post-procedure results, I observe that many more spinal nerve terminations remain disconnected.

"Damn!" I exclaim. "I don't understand what could have gone wrong."

I try to contact Jess to tell her I'm OK, but the communication network has been taken over by the government.

The display reads: "A state of emergency has been declared."

I can't send or receive messages.

"I wonder what that's all about," I ponder.

Just as I prepare to leave the lab, my communicator beeps momentarily, indicating that it is now Friday. As I approach the lab door, my communicator begins to beep continuously and a government-issued message appears on the flashing display.

"*WARNING. Imminent Danger. Take cover immediately and do not go outside. Remain in a safe location until further notice.*"

Having never seen such a message before and feeling anxious, I wonder what is happening and try to determine where in the lab I'll be safe. The walk-in refrigerator in the corner of the lab looks good to me.

When I open the refrigerator door, I feel a flood of cool air pass over me. My wheelchair barely fits into the narrow aisle between the shelves on either side, which are filled with temperature-sensitive chemicals and bottles full of preserved tissue samples. I realize that facing the back wall of the refrigerator is a bad idea if I want to get out, so I exit and then back in so I am facing the door. Not wanting to be trapped in the refrigerator with its stiff latch, I keep the door open a crack and wait to see what will happen next.

Nothing happens immediately, other than I can hear traffic noise and car horns in the distance. I suddenly realize I need to contact Aunt Ruth, my caregiver, so she'll know that I'm OK. However, my communicator displays a message stating that phone service is temporarily suspended.

Feeling increasingly apprehensive, I notice that the air is no longer cool in the refrigerator and the lab air temperature is rising sharply, so much so that I begin to perspire.

Outside, it has become very quiet. There's no more traffic noise, but the wind is getting much stronger. Opening the refrigerator door slightly, I can see daylight through the lab windows above the emergency exit on the far side of the lab. I also notice that the light intensity is increasing rapidly. In a few seconds, I have to look away or risk being blinded. Now it is getting really hot in the lab. It's so hot that, a short while later, I hear small explosions, which are probably the tires of cars out in the nearby parking lot exploding. The wind intensifies to a deafening roar, causing the building to shake and make creaking and groaning sounds as the wind increases to beyond hurricane-force levels.

This is no ordinary storm, I realize. *I wish I knew what was going on.*

After closing but not latching the refrigerator door, I hold onto the shelves on either side of me to steady them and prevent their contents from raining down on me. The daylight from the lab windows gradually darkens, likely from smoke, dust, and debris dispersed by the wind. Now I'm really scared.

I attempt to contact Aunt Ruth again, with no success. The whole building trembles as the wind continues to increase in intensity. A piece of debris shatters one of the lab windows, allowing airborne matter to enter, and the wind makes a loud howling noise. Just then, electrical power is lost and a battery-powered light mounted over the emergency exit switches on, leaving most of the lab, including the refrigerator, in darkness.

As a result of the intense heat and extreme wind, the building is fast losing structural integrity. A short while later, I hear a crashing sound as the floor above the lab partially collapses into the lab, with debris coming to rest against the refrigerator door. I try to push the door open, but it won't budge. I realize I'm trapped.

Outside, the temperature must be rising at an alarming rate, and I think I can hear distant oil wells and storage tanks exploding. I surmise that nearby businesses are probably being destroyed, the wind tearing them to pieces. Since I can smell smoke, what remains is probably bursting into flames that are fanned by the wind.

The cataclysmic event lasts well into the night. Only then does the wind finally begin to subside. I have no idea from one minute to the next if I'll survive or die.

The Research Institute building suddenly starts making more cracking and tearing noises, and all at once another portion of the building collapses with a roar that lasts several seconds. Choking dust enters the lab, so I cover my face with my shirt, but it still causes me to cough.

By early morning, I have slipped into an uneasy heat-induced sleep. I'm awakened a few hours later by the sound of voices calling to any survivors who may be trapped in the rubble.

One of the searchers must have navigated his way through the Research Institute hallways and around various pieces of debris because he arrives at my lab. With the lab entrance partially blocked by fallen debris and displaced lab furniture, he smashes the security lock and then forces the door open.

"Hello! Anyone in there? Can you hear me? Anyone there?" He says he is a military rescue worker looking for survivors to take to a rescue shelter a few miles away.

Having barely regained consciousness, I push on the refrigerator door while calling for help, knocking some of the debris to the floor.

"Help! Help! Over here!"

He hears my voice and navigates over the rubble until he reaches the refrigerator. Peering inside, he sees me in my wheelchair.

"Today is your lucky day," he says. "I could barely hear you. Are you OK in there?"

"Yes, just tired and weak," I reply, nodding. "Please get me out of here."

"Hi. I'm Josh. Hang tight, and I'll get some help so we can get this door open."

"Hi, Josh. I'm Kaylee."

Just then, his partner, Jim, appears. "Hey! We finally found a live one!"

"Hey. At last," Josh replies, nodding.

They work as a team to remove the rubble blocking the refrigerator door.

"We're going to have to carry you out of the building," Josh says. "All of the hallways are partially blocked, so I'll have to do it fireman style, but don't worry, I won't drop you."

"You better not!" I respond.

Josh lifts me out of my wheelchair and carries me toward the lab entrance.

"Stop!" I scream.

"Why?" Josh asks.

"I need my laptop from my desk. It's super important that I have it."

Jim asks me to point it out.

"Go straight ahead until I tell you to stop," I say. Jim complies and, using his flashlight to guide him, steps over, around, and through large pieces of debris, struggling to make his way to my cubicle.

"Stop. Now go six feet to your left. You'll see my nameplate on the divider."

"OK, I see it. Your desk collapsed and is resting on your laptop. Bad news. Your laptop is destroyed. It looks like the desktop fell on it, and it had a meltdown."

"OK. Thanks for trying," I reply, devastated.

"I found pictures that are probably of your parents and another one of an older lady and a plush blue-and-white whale," Jim says. "Do you want them?"

"Oh, yes, yes. Please bring them to me."

When Josh and I emerge from the building, my body slung over his shoulder, the sky is a smoky orange colour and I see extensive property damage evident in every direction.

"OK, Josh. You can put me down now," I say.

"Just hold on there," Josh replies. "Jim will have your wheelchair here in a minute."

Once seated in my wheelchair, I am awestruck by the level of damage that the Research Institute has suffered, and I wonder if any of my research can be salvaged. I feel stranded in a world that I do not recognize.

Jim hands me the photos and whale as well as a face mask with twin air filters. He tells me to put it on, as the air has become acidic and could potentially burn my eyes and lungs.

Josh and Jim remain standing next to me, waiting for our transport vehicle to arrive.

"So, what happened?" I ask.

"We had a close encounter with a solar fireball," Josh explains. "The sun had a surface eruption a long time ago that sent a molten fireball into space. A chunk of that fireball separated unexpectedly from the main mass, and as luck would have it, its trajectory caused it to travel in a parallel path with Earth, coming very close. So, what you are now experiencing is our 'new and improved environment.' You can't breathe without filtering the air, and almost every living thing is dead."

"What about our friends and relatives?" I inquire.

"Judging by the number of people we've found alive, I have a feeling that most did not survive," Josh replies.

I am in shock and momentarily speechless as I struggle to make sense of the situation.

"Thank you for rescuing me," I say.

Josh nods. "You're welcome. You're the only person we rescued today."

The sky is covered in a brown haze that makes the sun look like an orange ball, appearing and disappearing with the passing of smoke-filled clouds. Josh and Jim help me board the six-by-six military vehicle and then load up my wheelchair across from where I am seated. Josh joins Jim and the driver in the cab, and I find myself seated across from an elderly Asian lady. I smile at her, even though I know she can't see my smile because of the face mask.

"Hi. My name is Kaylee. What's yours?"

The lady doesn't respond. She just sits quietly with a blank stare, looking straight ahead.

I assume that either she doesn't speak English or maybe she is in shock. I look toward the cab. "Josh, where are we going?"

"We're taking you to a rescue shelter. Then, if you're deemed healthy enough to transfer, you'll be transported to an underground emergency shelter."

The route to the rescue shelter takes us near to where I live. I recognize one of the damaged houses. It is Mr. Sussman's house, and I can see the charred remains of his prized sports car with the carport collapsed on top of it, still smouldering.

As we approach the rescue shelter, I see two other empty military transports, two large white tents, and a school bus. Josh and Jim help me into my wheelchair.

I enter the first tent, which has a sign outside that says, "Register Here." Almost immediately, a volunteer approaches me.

"Here, fill out this registration form and then line up with the others over there," she says.

"Thank you," I reply. "I will."

"Would you like a flask of water?" she asks, holding one out.

"Yes, please."

I take a refreshing sip of water, noting that it is hot in the tent, which is, fortunately, not overly crowded. Only three people are ahead of me in line.

After registering, we are directed to the next tent, where we're to await further instructions. Soon, nineteen people are ready for transfer to the underground emergency shelter.

As we head over to the waiting school bus, it is evident that the bus suffered some firestorm damage, as some of the windows and the windshield are smashed, the loose glass removed. Two volunteers help me board and then stow my wheelchair for me.

During our trip to the emergency shelter, we must take an alternate route to pick up more passengers. The bus driver and some of the passengers work as a team to remove any debris that's blocking the road. Finally, after making several stops to clear debris and pick up other people, we reach the highway.

The highway is less treacherous than the road we just travelled, but it is still far from perfect, with sand drifts to navigate around and rubble everywhere. Communication services remain nonexistent. Many of the passengers try to contact loved ones, with no success.

As we approach a main highway intersection, we see flashing lights up ahead with various rescue vehicles and police cars offering assistance to anyone in need.

A female police officer waves for our bus to stop and then steps on board.

"You will not be able to return to the city, as most of the roads are impassable, and your dwellings have most likely been destroyed," she says. "For the time being, you'll be housed in the underground emergency shelter."

After travelling out of the city and traversing an arid landscape for another forty minutes, we can see the emergency shelter's entrance up ahead. The place is bustling with activity as volunteers, directed by some Federal Emergency Management Agency personnel, are busy setting up more tents. Numerous military trucks containing emergency supplies are being unloaded behind the storage tents, and newly arrived survivors are lined up in front of entrance B, waiting to be processed. The day is hot, and even though the atmosphere is clouded with dust and smoke, the sun is unrelenting in its attempt to scorch the landscape.

Since our group has completed the registration paperwork, we're directed into the shelter without delay. Upon entry, a man wearing a reflective vest instructs us to remove our face masks and deposit them in a nearby bin. The air is cool and refreshing after our hot bus ride, and the darkened atmosphere feels as if we're in a cave. Once our paperwork is reviewed, we're directed to a large, dimly lit waiting area until our living quarters are assigned.

I look around desperately to see if I recognize anyone, to no avail. Suddenly, a sick feeling in the pit of my stomach overcomes me as I realize that everyone that I know may be dead. My eyes start to well up with tears. Just then my name is called over the PA system, and a volunteer directs six of us down a series of corridors to our accommodations.

"I know it looks like we're in a labyrinth of underground passages, but you'll get used to finding your way around in no time."

Our room is small and is outfitted with six cots, each one with a shelf mounted above the headboard to store our few personal belongings. A toiletry kit, washcloths, and a bath towel are on each cot, and each cot is fitted with bedding and a pillow. The volunteer says that the room is meant to house four people, but more capacity is needed to prevent future arrivals from being forced to live in the hallways. Finally, she informs us that bathrooms and showers are down the hall.

"Excuse me. What is this place?" I ask.

"It's a place you never knew existed," she explains. "This facility was covertly constructed about ten years ago, when the threat of a deadly manmade global pandemic arose. It was designed to house key government officials, military personnel, and their families should the pandemic happen."

"I see," I reply, nodding. "We're so fortunate to have such a facility to house us with all that's going on now."

"You are so right," the volunteer says as she departs.

My cot is nearest to the doorway so it is easier for me to come and go. After a few minutes, I am alone in the room, with the others having gone off to explore. I gaze at the photos of my parents and Aunt Ruth, remembering snippets of my childhood, and then at my blue whale, which I have had since I was a child, then place it carefully on my shelf.

CHAPTER 3

At first, my life seems very different as the new underground lifestyle settles in. Many of the new arrivals volunteer to assist with the logistics of maintaining the wellness of thousands of people and their pets. Soon after the rescue shelter, which has its own regulated air supply, is fully operational, external atmospheric oxygen levels continue to drop sharply, drastically increasing the need for oxy-packs to be used at all times when outside of the shelter's climate-controlled environment.

Wanting to feel useful, I volunteer to help to refill oxygen canisters that attach to the oxy-packs' computerized breathing management modules. They dispense oxygen as needed to augment breathing. The oxy-packs deliver oxygen via a narrow, transparent tube fitted with slender clear breathing tubes that sit just below the nostrils. They remain with the wearer and are held in place with ear clips. It is critical that the oxy-packs are worn at all times when outside of the facility to prevent oxygen starvation, which can result in dizziness, shortness of breath, and eventual suffocation.

Over time, everyone seems to be acclimating to our new lifestyle. I haven't heard any news of my parents or Aunt

Ruth, including whether they survived the firestorm or where they might be if they did. My parents were living in Sacramento, and they may be in another rescue camp. Aunt Ruth would have been housed at the same facility as me if she survived. At the moment, with the exception of a large rescue shelter to the north, there is little in the way of communication between any distant rescue camps, with most communication networks being out of service.

A general meeting is called to establish a new government to oversee the operation of the underground rescue shelter and organize future projects. The residents of both rescue shelters are to vote for a new president and form a committee in both shelters to fill key government posts. We're told that the government will have a simplified structure that includes a president overseeing both shelters as well as the following posts for each shelter:

- chief medical officer;
- chief environmental officer;
- chief immigration officer;
- chief security officer;
- chief logistics and infrastructure officer; and,
- chief intercamp liaison officer.

In addition to recognizing that only one president will preside over both shelters, the rescue shelter to the north also agrees that all research activities are to be under the control of one research institute.

The presidential election happens two weeks later and includes one candidate from each shelter. We're immediately informed that the first item on the president's agenda is to assign resources to start preparations for building a new domed city for each of the rescue shelters to house and protect the general population. A man named Thomas Williams is the president-elect, and he calls a town hall meeting to take place the following day.

"The quality of life plus the safety and security of the populations of both camps is paramount," he says. "We know that living in the underground shelter is unsustainable for an indefinite time period. We're fortunate to have inherited a large stockpile of canned rations that were on site plus any food that can be recovered from Los Angeles to tide us over until the domed cities are completed.

"To that end, we have discovered a massive stockpile of material located in Los Angeles that was to be part of a government-funded project to build two futuristic cities. They will consist of multiple domes containing high-rise apartment buildings surrounding a central larger dome. Mr. Neufeld, the project's chief design engineer, said he believes the cities will afford us a comfortable standard of living in a climate-controlled environment. We'll be forming committees to organize the project and begin construction as soon as possible."

We're also told that one of the committees will appoint a chief science officer, who will be in charge of advanced research projects focusing on technologies that will ensure humankind's survival.

President-elect Williams assigns representatives for the committees for both shelters and proceeds to interview candidates, selecting those best qualified to fill the positions.

Two months later, I am returning from my day of volunteering when I happen to glance down the crowded hallway, I think I spot Jess in the distance. I manoeuvre my wheelchair through the crowded hallway, struggling to get close to her.

"Jess!"

Everyone within earshot turns and looks at me as Jess stops, then rushes over with tears in her eyes and gives me a big hug. We move off to the side of the hallway to chat.

"Kaylee! I can't believe it's you. It's really you! I've missed you so much."

"I missed you too! I thought you didn't make it. Let's go back to my room and catch up."

Minutes later, Jess and I are sitting across from one another, sipping some water.

"What have you been doing these past two months?" I ask.

"I've been working in the food distribution department. I guess we didn't see one another because your room is at the opposite end of the shelter from mine."

"Have you made any new friends?" I inquire.

"Yes! And they say there's a rebel camp not that far from here. The search for survivors ended, and they were left to fend for themselves. I hate the government."

"That seems so unfair. I heard that we're way over capacity, so that's probably why the search stopped."

Suddenly, Jess stands up. "I have to go."

"OK, bye," I reply, wondering if I've offended her.

Six months after the firestorm event, it is announced that the construction of the new multi-dome cities is well underway and that they will offer everyone a much-improved standard of living.

CHAPTER 4

One afternoon, after I return home from work, I find an envelope on my bed that arouses my curiosity. It is addressed to me and has a gold circular Research Institute crest on the back of it in the form of a self-adhesive seal. In the envelope is an invitation to meet with Robert Riggin, the newly appointed chief science officer, the next day at 2:00 p.m. I remember speaking to Robert occasionally a couple of times before the firestorm.

At 1:57 p.m. the following day, I am feeling apprehensive, wondering why Robert wants to see me. His office door opens, and after a brief exchange, a young man departs. Robert looks in my direction, smiles, then invites me in and sits in a chair next to me. He is a tall, thin man in his late fifties. He is balding, has a pleasant smile, and is wearing a dark-blue suit.

"Hi, Kaylee. It's so nice to see you. I know it's been a long time since we've spoken to one another. Tell me about yourself. How are you doing?"

"Before the firestorm, I was living with my Aunt Ruth, who became my caregiver when my parents moved to Sacramento because of my dad's work. I couldn't go to live with them because I was receiving experimental spinal treatments as a part of a research project. I haven't heard from Aunt Ruth or my parents since the firestorm, so I can only assume that they didn't survive."

"I'm so sorry to hear that your loved ones are missing," Robert says. "I have friends and relatives who are unaccounted for as well." He pauses a moment to shift gears before getting down to business. "It has taken us a long time to equip the lab with the necessary equipment to continue some critical projects that were interrupted by the firestorm. Now that we have a functioning lab, we need as many skilled people as we can get."

"What research opportunities are available?" I ask.

"In relation to supporting a high-priority project affecting the survival of humankind, we need to continue with tissue regrowth, DNA mapping, and an in-depth analysis of human brain function. Are you interested?"

I remain silent for a few seconds as I suddenly realize that this research is directly linked to developing the capability to repair my spinal cord.

"Yes. Yes, I would be delighted to join your research team," I say.

Robert smiles. "Great! My secretary will have some paperwork for you to fill out and then you can start in three days."

"Perfect. Thank you so much!"

Robert stands and shakes my hand. I can't wait to tell Jess about the meeting.

When I arrive a few minutes early to begin my first day at the new Research Institute, Robert greets me and wraps a security bracelet around my right wrist, then hands me three lab coats, which I place on my lap. After a short trip down a narrow hallway, we enter the lab using my security bracelet to make sure it works. Numerous benches are set up in rows filled with various pieces of test equipment, with aisles barely wide enough to accommodate my wheelchair. Tall dividers separate the rows of benches. As we turn the next corner, I see a familiar face.

"Logan!" I scream.

Logan turns. "Kaylee! Is it really you?"

He crouches down and gives me a big hug.

"Have you seen Tara or Katrina?" I ask.

Logan shakes his head. "No. You're the only person I've seen that I know since I arrived here."

I pull back and smile. "I'm so sorry to hear that, but I'm glad we'll be working together."

"We also have someone named Sarah. She started a week ago."

"Come with me," Robert says. "I'll show you our test chamber, complete with a slightly damaged operating table and the tissue-regrowth test fixture salvaged from the original Research Institute lab. We also saved some nano-probes."

"That's fantastic," I reply. "Now we won't have to re-engineer them. What about the data files?"

"Right now, we all have to share one computer terminal, so you can have a look at the salvaged memory modules and see what you can find," Robert replies. "That can be your first task, if you like."

"Yes. I hope at least some of the files are recoverable."

"For the time being, I'm the temporary lab manager until we find a suitable candidate," Robert says. "I'll leave you now. Logan can introduce you to Sarah."

When Robert departs, I use the computer terminal to scan the memory modules, some of which look pretty distressed. I spend the entire morning searching, but I don't find any of my secret tissue-regrowth files.

Sarah, Logan, and I have lunch together and get to know one another. I ask about her area of expertise related to the projects we're working on.

"Neurology," she replies. "Figuring out how the human brain works. Right now, I'm mapping the data-flow corridors within the cerebral cortex."

I realized right away what she is working on. Katrina was doing the same thing before the firestorm. I turn to Logan.

"I guess you haven't been mountain biking for quite a while."

"Well, actually, I have." Logan answers. "A group of us managed to recover some bikes and are using an empty storeroom with some piles of sand as moguls to ride over. We ride twice a week to stay in shape."

Searching the memory modules in the afternoon offers a spark of hope as a few of my files turn up. I'll have to check them when I start working on my tissue-regrowth research discreetly after hours.

Weeks turn into months, and between the three of us, we either recover or repeat as many of the original tissue-regrowth experiments as possible. We now have three working computer terminals and a salvaged large-scale server to work with.

After months of burning the midnight oil, I now believe that I'm ready to give the regrowth process an extreme test that will prove whether the methodology can be completely managed or not. My first thought is to have a lab monkey regrow its head on its abdomen, but that seems a little too "Frankensteinish," so I settle for an eye to grow on a monkey's abdomen. I know that the Research Institute would never approve of it, so I plan to carry out the experiment in secrecy.

A Rhesus monkey named Samey, one of three rescued from the California State University LA campus, is my favourite. When I open his cage, Samey jumps into my arms and hugs me. I reciprocate and kiss the top of his head.

"Samey, I have a very special task for you to perform," I whisper. "It's one that will eventually lead to my being able to walk. I promise that nothing harmful will be done to you."

Samey undergoes memory mapping, and I am able to capture all of the data required to regrow his left eye. The data is programmed into the salvaged aligning fixture to coordinate where the eye will be located, and a temporary transducer is strapped to his neck. The transducer has a communication cable that connects to the alignment fixture control module. I sedate Samey, shave his abdomen, and then place him on the operating table.

With the aligning fixture targeting Samey's abdomen, I inject intelligent nano-probes into Samey's abdomen at the site where the eye is to grow. A time-lapse camera will capture images of each stage of the procedure.

The first indication that a change to the abdomen is happening is a lump that forms at the target location. The lump gradually increases in size, and the abdominal skin seems to be stretched and discoloured. After a couple of hours, I doze off briefly. When I awaken, the regrowth process is complete, and Samey has a third eye, including an eyelid that opens and closes.

He awakens and seems to be in good health. The new eye looks and moves identically to his left eye, but I don't know if it actually works. I extend my index finger and move my hand toward Samey's third eye, and it blinks, as does his normal left eye. I block the normal left eye and hold a slice of banana in my hand close to the third eye, moving it from side to side. The third eye follows the slice of banana. Next, I unblock the normal left eye and reward Samey with several slices of banana. I'm so delighted, I can hardly contain myself.

The lab techs will be arriving in an hour, and I panic, not knowing how to hide Samey's third eye. I remember that the lab has small gowns and nightshirts for the monkeys, so I put a nightshirt on Samey. My plan works perfectly, and no one questions why Samey is wearing it. The experiment is a resounding success, and I am confident that the regrowth process will work to fix my spinal cord.

Two weeks later, Samey dies of natural causes. I'm saddened by the news, but I volunteer to look after the disposal of his corpse so his third eye will remain a secret forever.

CHAPTER 5

The next morning, Robert Riggin summons me to meet with him. I learn that I'll be transferred over to a new high-priority project and become the team lead for a human brain-to-computer interface. My advanced level of tissue-regrowth knowledge will be of great benefit in the development of a new technology called the uplink port.

I'll continue to advance my tissue-regrowth knowledge as time permits, though I'll have little free time due to my new workload.

Jess and I meet in the cafeteria after work, so she can tell me about some recent news.

"I know you'll be interested in this," Jess begins. "I saw a new posting asking for volunteers to relocate to the domed city construction site to help set up the food-production facility and other infrastructure. Do you want to go?"

"Sure, but my research is considered a top priority, so I'll have to ask for permission."

"Maybe we can work together with the plants and animals," Jess says.

"It would almost be like going on vacation, wouldn't it?" I reply.

The next day, I ask Robert for permission to volunteer to set up the food-production facility. He indicates that our research is important, but he also explains that he must supply at least three volunteers to the project, and I have been designated as one of them.

"But I thought my research is a high priority," I state.

"You're right. But that priority has been overridden by the need to finish the domed cities," Robert replies.

Jess and I depart to seek out the domed city volunteer office. As we approach, we see a short lineup next to the entrance. After a few minutes, we both approach the next available desk. The clerk is a middle-aged lady who does not look particularly enthused with her job. The office is cramped and warm with little in the way of ventilation.

"What do you want?" she snaps.

"We want to volunteer to help with the food-production facility at the domed city," I reply sheepishly.

The clerk looks me up and down. "I don't think wheelchairs are allowed at the construction site. It's too dangerous. Your friend can volunteer, but you can't."

I start to sob as Jess and I leave immediately. Then I look up at Jess, tears running down my cheeks. "I'm so sick and tired of being told what I can or can't do because of this stupid wheelchair! I'm going to get rid of this stupid thing and walk if it's the last thing I do!"

"I feel your pain," Jess replies. "Maybe we can try again tomorrow and talk to a different clerk."

The next day, after we finish our work, we head back to the volunteer office. Jess peeks inside to see if the same clerk is there, but someone else is at the desk: a petite blonde-haired young lady in a wheelchair!

As we enter, she's filing some paperwork into a multi-level tray on top of the cabinet behind her. When she's finished, she swivels around to greet Jess and me.

"Hi, my name is Lisa. How can I help you?"

"I'm Kaylee and this is my friend Jess," I reply. "We both want to volunteer to help set up the food-production facility in the domed city."

"Yes, you certainly can volunteer. I assume you two want to work as a team, which is perfectly fine. Please fill out the application form and then return it to me."

Excited, Jess and I waste no time completing the paperwork and returning it to Lisa. She tells us that we will receive details regarding our travel, living accommodations, and work assignments within the next few days.

"Jess, I'm so glad you suggested that we go back and try again," I say as we head home. "Lisa was so nice and didn't even question my being in a wheelchair. Hopefully my research will be able to help her to walk some day soon. What an amazing day! I can't wait to go!"

CHAPTER 6

A few weeks later it is 6:30 a.m., and I am in my room waiting for Jess, as we're about to embark on an adventure of epic proportions. I haven't been out of the rescue shelter for such a long time, and I can't wait to see the new city that will eventually be our home.

When Jess arrives, we depart immediately to be fitted with oxy-packs and tinted goggles to protect our eyes prior to exiting the shelter.

Once outside in the warmth of the sun, we notice that the sky is light orange. Our group of twenty is escorted to the shuttle bus transfer station to wait for our assigned bus to take us to the train station eighteen miles to the south. After what seems an eternity of travelling past the remnants of what was once a bustling city, the bus arrives at the train station. The station is crowded with people moving about in an organized level of chaos. The bus driver directs us to follow the instructions of a volunteer wearing a reflective orange-and-yellow safety vest.

After exiting the bus, Jess and I follow our guide past a number of holding zones until we arrive at holding zone thirty-three, which is identified by a large blue overhead sign with bright yellow graphics. Several train tracks pass by the train station, and a wide platform separates passenger traffic from freight trains. The train that Jess and I'll board has not arrived yet, allowing us time to take everything in.

"This place is so busy," I say, looking around. "I wonder if all of these people are volunteers like us."

Jess shakes her head. "Not sure. The train will definitely be full."

When the train arrives, we discover that the car that Jess and I are to board is equipped with a wheelchair ramp, which makes the boarding process much easier to accomplish. When all the passengers are on board, we depart. As the train pulls away, we're informed that our coach is equipped with breathable air, so oxy-packs are not required. While departing the train station, we pass by an extensive network of tracks where numerous box cars and flat cars are loaded with construction materials plus prefabricated modular apartments destined for the domed city. After that we can see a seemingly endless landscape of destroyed buildings and homes. Once we depart the city, we traverse a scenic mountain pass and then transition over into serene desert scenery. Two and a half hours later, we arrive at the construction site drop-off zone.

Jess and I put on our oxy-packs before a volunteer escorts us to our temporary living quarters, which consist of interconnected prefab buildings with a self-contained air supply. We're housed in a room that will accommodate up to a dozen people. The room has fabric dividers separating pairs of cots, offering some privacy. Our living quarters are outfitted with bedding and a kit on each cot with toiletries and a reusable drink container that is filled with refreshing ice-cold water.

Later that afternoon, we attend an orientation session to find out what our assigned tasks will be. Our group gathers in a school classroom, and Jess moves one of the desks out of the way to make room for my wheelchair. Two girls walk past, staring at me with a distasteful look on their faces.

"Haven't you been sent home yet?" one of them asks.

The girl is tall and thin with blonde hair and seems to have a self-important demeanour. The other girl is a short brunette who follows the first girl around like a puppy.

"No. I'm still here, and I'm not leaving!" I reply.

At that moment, Sylvia, our group leader, enters. She fastens a chart of the food-production facility to the wall and then stands with her back to it.

"OK, everyone, listen up. You're going to work together as a team to set up the food-production facility. It will be a hot working environment, so if you can't take the heat, let me know and you'll be transferred to another group."

The tall blonde girl stares at me as if I should drop out and move to another group. I stare back at her in defiance.

"As you can see on the chart, the food-production facility is divided into three parts," Sylvia continues. "We have a seedling department, a fruit and vegetable grow-op, and a livestock rearing division. It will take a few weeks to complete the setup. I'll give each of you your assignments along with an information package to read over. We start tomorrow."

Once the session concludes, the tall blonde glares at me and Jess as she and her friend walk out.

"See you tomorrow, losers," the blonde girl says. I find out later that her name is Chrissy and her friend's name is Samantha.

Early the next morning, Jess and I hurry off to the canteen for breakfast. There, we chat with other excited volunteers who are ready to see how their day will unfold. Shuttle buses transport us to the drop-off location next to the food-production facility. Jess and I have some difficulty getting the wheelchair from the bus drop-off through the soft gravel walkway to the ramp at the food-production facility's loading dock. I overhear Chrissy commenting about it to Samantha.

"What's she doing here?" Chrissy says. "She can't even make it to the building."

"You just worry about yourself," I retort. "We'll get there."

"You shouldn't have been allowed to come here in the first place!" Chrissy shouts.

"Go to hell!" I shout. By then, I'm pretty angry.

"Losers!" Chrissy shouts.

I look up at Jess as if to apologize for causing trouble.

"You're not making this difficult," she assures me. "We'll figure it out."

A construction supervisor overhears the confrontation and rushes over. By then, Chrissy and Samantha have departed.

"Hey there! What's the problem?" he asks.

"Those girls were making rude comments because we were having trouble getting the wheelchair through the gravel," Jess explains.

"Tell you what. I'll have my men lay down some sheets of plywood to make it easier for you to go to and from the food-production facility."

"Thank you!" I reply. "That would be great."

The construction site is buzzing with activity, with vehicles carrying people and building materials to various locations across the vast area. Jess and I wait at the food production facility service entrance for further instructions and watch as scaffolding is set up to facilitate the installation of the hybrid-dome covering for the larger central dome while cranes stack prefabricated dwellings on top of each other to create high-rise living accommodations and office space. Most of the dome's support buildings are in place, with finishing work taking place on the building next to the food-production facility. The dome's supporting structures are being readied for the installation of additional high-rise apartment buildings contained in smaller domes that surround the central dome.

Our group leader ushers us into the massive empty structure and puts Jess and I to work assembling tables that will grow fruit and vegetable plants from seeds.

At first, I'm frustrated by Jess's lack of mechanical aptitude, but after gaining some experience, we work together like a well-oiled machine.

"So, working for the government isn't that bad, is it?" I ask.

"No, but I still think they want to control everything we do. It's called slavery."

"Oh, come on. We need food to survive, don't we? Isn't that why we're here?"

Jess shrugs. "I suppose."

Later that day, when we head back to the shuttle bus stop, Jess and I smile and wave to thank the construction supervisor for his assistance with the pathway. Soon we return to our temporary home away from home.

Even though the working conditions inside the food-production facility are uncomfortably hot, we enjoy our time there immensely. Jess and I work there for two months. Then one day, we see Chrissy and Samantha approaching.

"Hey, how's it going, losers?" Chrissy asks. "Aren't you done putting tables together yet?"

"You must be lost!" I reply. "Can we help you find your way back to your group?"

At that moment, an overhead water pipe springs a leak during a water pressure test, soaking all four of us. We purposely remain under the shower of water that feels so cool and refreshing, laughing at one another as we cavort about. The floor is soon soaked, and Chrissy slips and falls, ending up on her hands and knees next to me. With both of us soaking wet, we stare at each other for a moment.

"Take my hand," I offer. "I'll help you up."

Chrissy doesn't know what to say. She hesitates for a moment.

"I don't need your help. I can look after myself!" Chrissy says as she stands up.

Chrissy and Samantha are about to leave and turn to look at Jess and I.

Chrissy shouts, "Bye, losers!"

Jess and I look at one another and shake our heads.

"Some people will never change," I say.

"Doesn't seem likely. Go figure," Jess replies.

That night, the food-processing facility's cooling system is turned on, offering a pleasant climate-controlled environment for the plants and livestock that are soon to arrive.

Finally, with all of the setup complete, the chickens, turkeys, and rabbits are scheduled to arrive in the afternoon. Jess and I are beyond excited and spend the morning double-checking the automated watering and feeding systems to make sure everything is functioning properly.

When the livestock arrives, Jess and I are assigned to help introduce the creatures to their new home. We spend the rest of the day having a wonderful time interacting with the young turkeys, two-week-old chicks, and baby bunnies.

Having completed our volunteer assignment, I am excited to return by train to the underground rescue shelter and continue with my research. Jess does not share my excitement.

CHAPTER 7

We learn that while we were away, the domed cities were given names. The one we will occupy is now known as New Washington, and the other is to be known as New Los Angeles.

Six months later, my research has advanced to the point where I am planning a major experiment in an attempt to fix my spinal cord. I receive notification that most of the population of the underground rescue shelter will be moving into our assigned apartments in New Washington. This is exciting news, and we can't wait to be living in a less-cramped, breathable environment and leading a more or less normal life. I hope that New Washington will have a research facility.

As we board a shuttle bus, Jess and I look upon the rescue shelter for the last time.

"I am not going to miss the rescue shelter. How about you?" I ask.

"I won't miss the rescue shelter, but I will have to find a way to access the darknet," Jess replies.

Then, we have to endure the heat of the day as we travel to the train station. The platform is packed with people as

Jess manoeuvres my wheelchair around and through the mass of people to our boarding zone. The train pulls up to the station, aligning the cars at the loading zones. I'm permitted to board first, using the wheelchair ramp.

Shortly after departure, we remain quiet and stare at the familiar scenery as we ascend the mountain pass, and soon the topography gradually changes to wide-open spaces in an arid environment.

Before long, we see our new home looming in the distance. New Washington consists of multiple domes extending up from the desert landscape.

I ask, "Hey, Jess. We're almost there. Are you excited?"

"Not really," Jess responds.

"Oh, c'mon show some enthusiasm," I suggest.

Jess replies, "I'd rather live in the commune and be free."

The city becomes much more imposing as the train nears its destination. Excitement builds as we approach. I overhear other passengers express their eagerness.

"Oh, look! Up ahead. It's our new home!"

"Look at the domes. Aren't they huge?"

When we arrive at the New Washington train station, we're told to put on our oxy-packs. Then we're directed to buses that will drop us off next to a walkway that takes us into our dome.

Jess assists me up the ramp and into our assigned dome. I stop briefly to remove my oxy-pack, depositing it in a bin. Then I take in the magnitude of our new home. The air smells so fresh, and I am relieved to know that no longer do I have to endure the rescue shelter's cramped quarters and lack of daylight. Also, no more putting up with snoring from a couple of my roommates!

"Jess, isn't this place amazing?" I ask.

"If you say so," Jess says snidely.

The dome is filled with high-rise buildings surrounding a small courtyard, and a wide walkway connects us with the even larger central dome. At the centre of the courtyard is a fountain, and elevated flowerbeds are situated around the perimeter. The courtyard is populated with a few benches as well so people can sit and enjoy our living quarters.

Our new home is located in a high-rise structure known as Building C. Jess and I are sharing the apartment just as we had hoped we could. The apartment is pure luxury compared to the underground shelter.

"Oh, Jess, look at our bedrooms. So much space. And our kitchen. The refrigerated pantry is huge and all of the meals that have been prepared for us. We don't have to cook anything," I exclaim.

Jess replies, "I will admit, this place isn't half bad."

After exploring our new home, we sip on a drink and chat for a while. Then we unpack our belongings in our separate bedrooms and freshen up with a long shower. There is much to learn about our new home and new lifestyle. After supper, Jess and I plan to go out to visit the central dome.

After a short walk, we enter the central dome. We're awestruck by its size. There's a tree-lined promenade with flowerbeds interspersed throughout the park-like setting. We traverse the walkways, observing various tall structures that surround the promenade and visit one of the sidewalk cafés situated around the promenade's perimeter. After relaxing in the central dome, we return to our apartment and soon head off to bed for a well-deserved sleep.

The next morning, after enjoying our first breakfast in our new home, we decide to go for another walk in the central dome, and after travelling many of the walkways, we visit one of the cafés and enjoy a beverage.

"Well, I guess we made it," Jess said. "Our bigger and better prison."

"Oh, Jess. This is so much better than the underground shelter. Why are you so pessimistic?"

Jess scoffs, "Prisons have different shapes and sizes, but they're still prisons. Just like when I was a kid, my parents locked me in a room for hours so I wouldn't *bother* them."

"That's terrible," I reply, trying to soothe her bitterness. "I like our apartment, though. Now all I have to figure out is what to do with my time. There just has to be a research lab here somewhere."

CHAPTER 8

I'm not sure what the future will hold for me seeing as the only research facility is back in the underground shelter. However, one day shortly after arriving in New Washington, I receive an invitation to meet with Robert Riggin, who is now the chief science officer at the New Washington Research Institute. I couldn't be more delighted. I have to call Jess.

"Jess, you won't believe what just happened!"

"Calm down, girl, before you burst! What's up?"

"I just received an invite to meet with Robert Riggin here at the new Research Institute! I thought I was destined to be stuck in my wheelchair for the rest of my life. Now I'm hoping there will be some form of ongoing medical research so that my spinal cord can be fixed."

"I'm so happy for you. Let me be the first to know how the meeting goes."

"Thanks! I will!"

Feeling super excited but also nervous, I prepare to depart for my interview. When I exit Dome C and enter the panoramic central dome, the Research Institute building is straight ahead in the distance. The promenade is full of people navigating through the labyrinth of walkways to reach their workplaces.

When I enter the Research Institute's high-ceilinged foyer, I notice that every sound echoes, reminding me of the caves I visited with my parents a few years ago. The receptionist notifies Robert that I have arrived. A few minutes later, Robert comes to the foyer to greet me.

"Welcome, Kaylee. I've been looking forward to meeting with you."

After we shake hands, I am feeling a little more at ease.

"Thanks for inviting me," I reply.

"How do you like living in New Washington so far?" Robert asks.

"I love it here. My apartment is perfect, and the meals are great."

Robert smiles. "That's good. The reason for our meeting today is to offer you a placement in the medical research program as a member of our advanced medical research team."

"I accept!" I reply almost immediately. "I wasn't sure if there was any sort of research facility here in New Washington until I received your invitation."

"We were able to recover a significant amount of computer hardware from Los Angeles," Robert explains, "and we have created a state-of-the-art facility that is second to none. It is critical to the survival of humankind that advances in emerging new technologies continue."

"I would be honoured to be a member of the advanced medical research team."

"I've always thought that you have exceptional potential and will prove to be an outstanding research scientist," Robert says.

I smile. "I appreciate your confidence in my abilities. I'm hoping in the future that, for example, advances in tissue-regeneration research will enable the human body to repair injuries or defects. Perhaps one day, we'll have the capability to fix my spinal cord so I can walk."

"I can see why you're so highly motivated, and I respect that," Robert says. "Very well then. Do you have any further questions? If not, I'll walk you back to the foyer. We'll contact you in a few days and present you with your welcome package."

"Actually, I have one more question. I see that a new building is under construction beside the Research Institute. What's it for?"

"So far all of the government-issued bulletins have informed the public of a new form of entertainment that will be unlike anything they have ever experienced. I can tell you that the Dream Palladium is to house the new Infinium computer system to archive all research files and government records. It is the computer interface link for the uplink ports soon to be worn by the entire population."

"So, what's the new form of entertainment?" I ask.

"The purpose of the Dream Palladium is going to be revealed on a Helen Dijon talk show coming up soon. That's all I can tell you for now."

Robert escorts me to his office door and bids me farewell.

Feeling like I'm floating on air, I join Jess at our favourite sidewalk café for a late lunch.

"Hey, how did your interview go?" Jess asks.

"Great! I'm to become a member of the advanced medical research team."

"Oh, I'm so glad for you! Even if you're working for the government again. A few days ago, you seemed to be like a lost sheep, not knowing what to do."

"You know why I want to work at the Research Institute," I reply. "I'll walk one day. You'll see."

"Here, I made this for you."

Jess hands me a small gift wrapped in a plain cloth.

"What is it?"

"Open it and see."

I open it, and a woven pink-and-purple bracelet drops onto the table.

"It's a 'best friends forever' bracelet. I used our favourite colours. If we ever become separated, it will be a reminder of our forever friendship. I have one too," she adds, showing me hers.

"Thank you," I say, smiling. "It's beautiful, and I'll always wear it."

I feel like I'm on top of the world as I prepare for my first day at the Research Institute, where I'll be working with some of the most talented minds ever assembled under one roof.

When I arrive, Robert welcomes me and two other new hires, who turn out to be lab technicians.

After a brief orientation session, where we receive our security bracelets for admittance into the Research Institute lab, he introduces us to the other members of the research team.

Initially, I am assigned to assist with the ongoing human-brain coding experiments. No time is wasted bringing me up to speed. As an added bonus, working well into the night on my own time, I am able to unravel some of the bizarre human-brain coding mysteries.

Robert is so impressed with my capabilities that he places me in charge of a new mind-mapping project and assigns two lab techs to work with me.

Upon completion of that project, Robert tells me that I'll be transferred over to a new high-priority project where I'll become the team lead. My advanced level of tissue-regrowth knowledge will be of great benefit in the development of a new technology called the uplink port. In addition, I'll continue to advance my tissue-regrowth knowledge as time permits, though I have little extra time due to my new workload.

My team of biogenetic engineers, software developers, and I work tirelessly to create an incredible new electronic device that will be of great benefit to humankind.

CHAPTER 9

Robert is invited to be a guest on the Helen Dijon talk show to tell the public about a new form of entertainment that is being developed. He asks me if I would be willing to join him to explain how the uplink port interfaces with the human brain.

Jess agrees to accompany me. She thinks she's my coach, prompting me with all the do's and don'ts of an interview. She makes me laugh.

"C'mon, Kaylee, we have to get going."

"Coming! Just finishing my makeup."

I am dressed in a black outfit consisting of a short-sleeve top, tight-fitting slacks, and a gold necklace. I'm hastily applying dark-blue eyeshadow. Finally, I brush my long golden-brown hair to curve gently around one side of my face and descend past my shoulder. I'm finally ready.

"Wow, you look amazing!" Jess exclaims when she sees me. "Aren't you nervous? Do you think you'll freeze if she asks you a question? You know how shy you are."

"No, I'm fine. Well, I'm a little nervous. No, maybe a lot nervous. I'll know better after the interview. Let's go."

Virtual Destiny

The Helen Dijon television show airs at 7:00 p.m., Monday through Friday. She interviews guests regarding various newsworthy topics of interest.

"Hi, my name is Helen Dijon, and I'm so glad you could join me this evening," Helen says into the camera to begin the show. "Tonight, we will be discussing the much-anticipated grand opening of the Dream Palladium. Our guests this evening are none other than the chief science officer of the New Washington Research Institute, Doctor Robert Riggin, and lead biological engineer, Miss Kaylee Parker. Let's give them a warm welcome."

Applause ensues as Robert wheels me out onto the stage.

"It's a privilege to have you two take time out of your busy schedules to be with us tonight," Helen says.

Robert smiles. "Thanks for inviting us."

"So, Robert, tell us about some of the recent developments at the institute," Helen says.

"We have a number of interesting projects underway, and one of the best known is the much-publicized Dream Palladium, which is currently under construction."

"Can you explain the purpose of the Dream Palladium?" Helen asks.

"Of course. The Dream Palladium is a venue that offers a new form of entertainment where the audience participates by witnessing a dreamer's dream as if they were actually there. A key feature of the Dream Palladium is the audience's ability to mentally connect with selected dreamers via their uplink ports utilizing our new Infinium computer system. Participants will choose a dreamer and be an invisible observer of their dream."

"OK. So, a few people dream and the audience will witness their dream," Helen says. "Did I get that right?"

Robert nods. "Correct. In addition, they are also emotionally connected to the dreamer they choose to follow. If the dreamer is scared or in danger, for example, the audience feels the same emotions as if they are there."

"How is that possible?"

Robert turns to me. "I'll let Kaylee answer that question."

"Kaylee, thank you for joining us today," Helen says. "I understand that you are the lead biological engineer for this project. Can you please tell us what sort of new technology we're dealing with?"

Feeling self-conscious, I hesitate for a few seconds. "Um, sure. I'm but one member of a team of highly skilled engineers who have overcome many obstacles to create this new technology. The uplink port is designed primarily to be a computer interface between our brain and the new Infinium computer system. The uplink port will continuously monitor our health and flag any issues that arise. The uplink port will also enable us to control the mental interaction taking place between the dreamer and audience members' brains. The ports are very small and will be located on our necks behind our right ears. The devices can send and receive data. Dreamers will be generating and transmitting their dreams to the audience, and the audience can choose a dreamer to follow. I hope I'm not making this too difficult to understand."

I pause briefly to allow the audience to process the information conveyed thus far.

Continuing on: "This interactive experience is now possible using the incredibly powerful new Infinium computer system in conjunction with the software platform we have developed. The audience will not only see what the dreamer sees, they will also experience other sensory inputs such as audio, smell, emotional responses, and feelings such as hot or cold along with their chosen dreamer."

"That sounds incredible," Helen replies. "Are the dreams manipulated or managed in any way?"

"We do monitor the dreams carefully," Robert says. "We use 'happy gas' as a stimulant along with the dreams being managed using computer software to keep them on track."

"Oh yes, happy gas," Helen says. "Best invention ever! Audience, do you agree?"

Applause erupts again.

"If I remember correctly, happy gas was invented by a scientist who lost his son to drugs," Helen says. "So, to retaliate, he invented a gas that can give anyone an unbeatable high but is non-addictive. He put the drug lords out of business instantly and drug addiction vanished. All I know is that it sure cures a headache in a hurry."

"Yes, it is also used for medical purposes," Robert explains. "For the Dream Palladium application, the gas is used to stimulate the dreamers and audience members' minds. It places them in an elevated conscious state to enhance their experience."

Helen claps her hands. "This all sounds so exciting. When will the Dream Palladium open?"

"The grand opening is to take place on June 30," Robert declares, "and invitations to attend the grand opening have already been distributed."

"The Dream Palladium experience sounds truly amazing, and we can't wait for the grand opening," Helen says. "Thank you both once again, Robert and Kaylee, for joining us today."

The audience offers a final round of applause as the show draws to a close.

CHAPTER 10

A government issued e-bulletin informs the population of New Washington that all residents are required to be fitted with an uplink port. My appointment is at 10:00 a.m. tomorrow morning. Jess, who has yet to receive her uplink port, agrees to accompany me to the medical centre.

The e-bulletin explains that the purpose of the device is twofold. First, it is to monitor the recipient's health and send that information to a database located in the New Washington Infinium computer system. Second, it allows the Infinium computer to send information, as required, to the person's brain to take any self-administered corrective action as deemed necessary should any health issues arise. In some instances, the body can heal itself through brain stimulation, but in others, external intervention may be required by a healthcare professional.

One of the software engineers has told me about a hidden non-publicized feature of the uplink port. Its purpose is to transmit everything people see, say, think, and do to the Infinium computer system. It also tracks everyone's movements.

I found this feature of the uplink port quite disturbing, as it was not stated as an objective at the outset of this project.

Maybe Jess is right after all. It would seem to me that the government has purposely voided our right to intellectual privacy.

"C'mon, Kaylee, it's time to go to the medical centre."

"Coming! I'll be out in a minute."

Leaving Dome C, we enter the central dome and take the elevator to the upper walkway that will take us to the medical centre.

As we approach the medical centre entrance, we see the Dream Palladium, which is under construction. We proceed to the fourth floor, where the receptionist welcomes us and asks us to have a seat in the waiting room. A few people are sitting quietly watching a video monitor. A few minutes later, one of the nurses summons Jess and I to follow her.

"Are you nervous?" Jess asks.

"Yes, a little."

"Don't worry," Jess says. "I'll be with you the whole time."

We enter a treatment room, where a large ominous-looking machine sits in the corner. A reclining chair is in the middle of the room. Two video monitors are suspended above the chair. The nurse instructs me to sit in the reclining chair and hands me a small cup half filled with an orange liquid to drink that will help me relax prior to being put into a deep sleep. Jess makes herself comfortable in the viewing room. It has a large window. I overhear the nurse reassuring Jess that everything will be fine.

Then the nurse returns to the treatment room.

"Hi, my name is Becky, and I'll be taking care of you while your uplink port is being installed. Do you have any questions or concerns?"

"How long will it take?" I ask.

"About forty-five minutes. Any more questions?"

"No. I'm ready."

Becky places a face mask with a happy gas inlet tube over my face. A few seconds later, I am in a deep sleep, ready for the installation of my uplink port.

Prior to my appointment, I watched a video presentation of the uplink port installation. It starts with the nurse leaving the treatment room momentarily and returning carrying a small package. Then she powers up the machine in the corner. Next, the nurse uses an alcohol swab to sanitize the area on the patient's neck where the new uplink port will be installed. Then the nurse positions the uplink port installation fixture next to the patient and presses the "start" icon on a touchscreen. That sets in motion a robotic arm to move the uplink port adapter, located at the end of the arm, to a pre-set location over the neck near the patient's right ear.

Once the overhead video displays are active, one shows the patient's vital signs, and the other shows the area of the neck where the port will be mounted. The nurse opens a small package and affixes the uplink port onto an adapter located at the end of the robotic arm. The uplink port is a flesh-coloured disc that is three quarters of an inch in diameter with a raised centre and is three sixteenths of an inch thick.

An image of a cross section of my neck appears on the overhead monitor as well as the monitor on the machine, showing many lighter and darker blood vessels. The robotic arm projects a small circle of blue light, two centimetres in diameter with intersecting vertical and horizontal red lines, onto my neck. The image visually indicates the exact position where the uplink port is to be located.

The nurse watches as the computer-controlled arm positions itself in exactly the right location. A shaft with the new port attached begins to extend from the arm toward my neck and soon brings the port into contact with my skin. Then the port attaches itself to my neck tissue by extending thin barbed fish-hook-like fingers into the tissue. Next, a series of fine needles extend into the flesh and release tiny self-directed transducers, called intelligent nano-probes, that use the circulatory system to navigate to precise locations within my brain. They will attach themselves to major information corridors within my brain and use plasma-transmission technology to wirelessly move data. The nano-probes are capable of sending and receiving data to and from the uplink port. They can also issue commands to the brain originating from the new Infinium computer system that can't be overridden by the individual. This feature is necessary to prevent people from interrupting critical life-saving procedures that may be administered.

Finally, some of the uplink port needles withdraw from my neck tissue, completing the installation of the port. The robotic arm and adapter withdraw from my neck, and the nurse moves the uplink port installation fixture over to the corner of the room. The installation goes perfectly, and I'll be asleep for a little while longer. Some brief diagnostic sequences need to be completed. The diagnostic computer, which is on another rolling cart, is moved into position next to me, and the nurse connects a communication cable from the diagnostic computer to the uplink port. The diagnostic computer is configured to activate each patient's online account, followed by a series of diagnostic tests to verify that the port is functioning properly. Once all parameters are checked, the port is brought online, and the nurse checks that the information fed back is accurate to verify that the port is capable of sending and receiving data.

When a patient is awakened, they are transferred to a recovery room. The nurse ensures that the patient is doing well with no ill side effects from the installation and then releases the patient, concluding the procedure.

After my installation is completed and I finish my recovery, Jess and I go for lunch at our favourite sidewalk café. Once we're seated, Jess decides to interrogate me.

"It's a conspiracy, you know. I've heard that the government uses them to spy on people without their knowing."

"Oh, c'mon," I reply in exasperation. "Look around. There are security cameras everywhere, and your communicator tracks every piece of information you send or receive. So, what difference does it make if you have an uplink port?"

"Because! Now they're literally in your brain. You can be made to do anything they want. Maybe even kill people they perceive to be the enemy."

"Now you're going too far! You've been spending too much time talking to your rebel friends. Let's put this topic aside so we can enjoy our lunch."

Jess reluctantly agrees. "OK. But I'm never having one of those ports on me. Never!"

Back at my apartment, I watch a replay of the Helen Dijon interview and am not impressed with my stage presence. Being shy and self-conscious about my appearance, I felt awkward, and it shows.

CHAPTER 11

My communicator beeps with a government-issued message displayed in red text.

"Please check your email for an important notification that requires your immediate attention."

The introductory paragraph states that the Dream Palladium's grand opening is planned for June 30. Then I am instructed to open the attachment. I'm puzzled and yet curious as to what the attachment may contain.

As the message opens, a logo appears that I have never seen before. The letters "DP" appear in gold in the middle of the display on a black background along with the words "Your Invitation" in white text. In a few seconds, a lavishly decorated page appears with black scripted text on a white background with colourful decorative graphics surrounding the border.

"You are invited to attend the Dream Palladium's grand opening as a VIP guest. To introduce this new and unforgettable concept in entertainment, you have been chosen to be one of a group of dreamers whereby your dream will be witnessed by members of the audience. The grand opening will take place on

June 30, and you'll receive further details soon. This is an event that you don't want to miss!"

My first reaction to the invitation is, "Why me?" Then after giving this some thought, I realize that Robert probably offered my name to the dreamer selection committee. Just then Jess stops by.

"Guess what?" I say. "I've been selected to be a dreamer at the grand opening of the Dream Palladium. I'm not sure if I'm excited or nervous. I don't like being in front of a lot of people."

"Are you kidding? So, you're going to allow them to invade your brain and manipulate it while you're on drugs for the sake of entertainment. I can't believe that you would be willing to do this. Are you going?" Jess replies.

"Yes, I am. Jess, you are blowing this way out of proportion. It's not as if they intend to turn me into a robot or something. Besides, I think Robert Riggin expects me to go, so I don't really have a choice."

"Sorry, I don't have one of those ports so I can't follow your dream. Have to go to work. See you later."

"Hey, don't work too hard."

"Never do," Jess replies, heading out.

CHAPTER 12

The Dream Palladium control room is buzzing with activity as all the operators check and recheck system functionality, and stress levels are running high. Caroline Wallace, the technical director of operations, is feeling strained.

"System check!" she says. "How are we looking, Steve? Don't give me any bad news! Today has to go perfectly."

Steve Hamm is the technical systems guru responsible for his team of software experts. He handles the Dream Palladium's operating parameters in a calm and reassuring manner.

"All systems are up and running," he says. "Minor technical difficulties with a few of the audience seats. Seems to be in one small area, and the techs are looking into it. The main stage is a go. Dreamer docking is also a go, and we ran a final simulation just an hour ago to verify that the Infinium dreamer communication network is functioning correctly," Steve assures Caroline. "Lighting and special effects are all set up and ready to go. All online services, customer services, and concessions show a green-light status and are fully operational. My team is the best! They're doing an amazing job."

"Just let me know if anything comes up that needs my attention," Caroline says.

"We have everything under control," Steve replies, smirking. "What could go wrong?"

Caroline glares at Steve as she continues on her way.

The big day has finally arrived. The other dreamers and I arrive at the Dream Palladium administrative entrance at 9:00 a.m. and are escorted via an underground passage to a private reception area. The room is equipped with soft and comfortable blue high-back, simulated-leather chairs that face a large oval table in a dimly lit room. The floor covering is plush black, blue, and white carpet, and simulated oak wood grain panelling is digitally displayed on the illuminated walls. The Dream Palladium logo is presented prominently in the middle of the table. Upon arrival, I notice that one of the chairs has been removed, presumably to accommodate my wheelchair. We're provided with snacks, and each guest is supplied with a tablet containing orientation information.

A Dream Palladium hostess appears on a wall monitor.

"Hello, and welcome to the Dream Palladium's grand opening. My name is Christie, and I'll be coordinating your activities for the day. Let's start with an introductory video explaining what will take place today."

The video explains that the dreamers can use their tablet to select the sleepwear style they prefer and can keep them as a souvenir. They will also receive a T-shirt and a digital plaque commemorating the occasion.

"Today you'll experience the ultimate virtual experience where your dreams are going to be shared with an audience of twenty-five hundred participants," Christie says. "Using your uplink ports, we can connect your dream experience with the conscious state of audience members, and they will invisibly follow your dream as if it were their own."

Following a short break, the instruction video takes us through each stage of our dream experience. The uplink port will transmit our dreams to the host computer, which in this case is the New Washington Infinium computer system.

"You will rest comfortably in your individual reclining seats located on centre stage," Christie continues. "Happy gas will put you quickly into a deep sleep whereupon your dream will commence immediately. Dreaming will continue for about an hour, and you'll awaken refreshed with no after effects or residual discomfort. Following your dream session, each dreamer can choose from a variety of individually selected rewards as a thank-you gift for participating today. That's it."

After our orientation session is complete, we're taken on a behind-the-scenes tour to learn more about the fascinating new facility.

We follow Christie to a freight elevator that takes us up one floor to the main entrance. and we gather in the centre of the large foyer.

"The Dream Palladium is a spectacular piece of technical engineering and is an architectural masterpiece. It is an oblong building capable of comfortably entertaining five thousand people," Christie states. "The interior features a translucent ceiling supported by upward curving structural beams."

Christie goes on to explain that the beams terminate at a spherical dome containing a series of holographic images depicting roving brainwaves that look similar to the aurora borealis. The beams intersect high above the atrium to symbolize that we're all part of an interconnected network where minds can now literally join together. The Dream Palladium's elongated mushroom-shaped exterior will glow as the sky darkens with a soft blue-green luminescence.

"As you may notice," Christie says, continuing our tour, "the panoramic rotunda has white walls with decorative pillars and a high ceiling, and the floor is carpeted in a plush blue, black, and white twist-pattern carpet that transitions over to an off-white ceramic tile floor. Please follow me."

The tiled floor continues around the perimeter of the walled-off auditorium. Proceeding down the broad promenade, we see the available goods and services, ranging from childcare to ice-cold beer, with many food-delivery outlets visible on the left side of the walkway.

"I could use an ice-cold beer right now and maybe some breakfast too," a dreamer named Rusty says. Everyone laughs.

Kiosks are scattered throughout the expansive open area, offering visitors information pertaining to available services and upcoming events. Continuing on, we see a large seating area where visitors can enjoy dining in an atrium that is furnished with trees and elevated planter boxes overflowing with tropical flowers. The high greenish-blue translucent ceiling creates an outdoor-like atmosphere to enjoy. Tables are distributed throughout the atrium to accommodate guests.

"If you look at the centre of the food court seating area, you'll notice that the floor is transparent, and various videos from International Geographic are presented below the transparent floor, offering archived views of wildlife in their natural habitat," Christie points out. "Other forms of graphic content may be shown as well."

As we continue on, we're surprised to see that various images are projected onto a fine mist of liquid forming a vertical curtain, creating a curved, elongated screen located next to the inside wall that separates the auditorium seating area from the food court.

Next, we follow Christie to the auditorium. The seating areas are all colour coded with illuminated colour bands wrapped around the exterior of the upright seat backs to enable people to find their seats quickly. She tells us that the circular centre stage has a programmable illuminated floor that is now dark blue. The perimeter of the stage is illuminated with a thin band of vibrant blue light. A series of overhead displays are suspended over centre stage, forming a circle and providing the audience with information regarding upcoming events, time of day, and a countdown to the event's start. The wall behind the seating area is illuminated as well and is currently set to dark purple.

When visitors arrive at their assigned seats, they make themselves comfortable by setting the individual comfort parameters to their liking. Each seat has a transparent bubble-like canopy that encloses the audience member's head and chest area. Once they are seated, their uplink port links them to the Infinium computer network. The canopy is necessary because a small continuous dose of happy gas is required to ensure that guests maintain an elevated mental state of immersion. Finally, Christie explains that each visitor is monitored throughout their interactive dream experience to ensure they are physically well and fully engaged.

After our tour, we return to the conference room. A clock in the upper-right corner of the monitor shows that it is 1:00 p.m. The monitor also shows that guests are beginning to arrive at the Dream Palladium's main entrance.

After lunch, we're escorted to an elevated VIP skybox overlooking the audience and facing the stage. The grand opening begins at 3:00 p.m. sharp, as it is to be televised live to New Washington and New Los Angeles viewers. At 2:00 p.m., the invited guests start to stream into the auditorium.

The stage is empty, and the illuminated floor remains dark blue with tiny blue-and-white Dream Palladium logos randomly scattered here and there. The circular video display surrounding the overhead control centre suspended over centre stage shows various exterior and interior images of the Dream Palladium under construction.

Pre-show entertainment is provided by various musicians, including a guitarist, violinist, a pianist, and, finally, a five-piece ensemble that plays classical music. Audience members chat amongst themselves as excitement builds in anticipation of what is to come.

The overhead displays switch off, and the auditorium lights gradually darken. Seat-back illumination decreases to allow the audience to focus on the stage. Except for a blue band of light extending around the perimeter of the stage, the auditorium is completely dark and the audience is eerily quiet. The silence is broken when Alex, the master of ceremonies, magically appears on stage under a spotlight. He is the host of a popular game show and is well known to most of the guests.

"Welcome to the grand opening of the Dream Palladium!" Alex begins. "What a magnificent facility we have, made possible by a team of outstanding individuals. This project has gone from concept to reality in an extremely short period of time. Some of the images that are being displayed on the overhead monitors give us some insight into how this masterpiece of architectural design and technology has come to fruition. Doctor Robert Riggin, chief science officer of the New Washington Research Institute, will be presenting further details of the operating capability of the Dream Palladium a little later in the program. Now let me introduce to you our own New Washington Dance Academy dance troupe."

The stage goes completely dark. A few moments later, under subdued lighting of varying colours, the stage floor is transformed into a virtual lake with rippling water. Fog flows across the stage, and a mixture of twenty-two male and female ballet dancers offer their impression of a moonlight dream. Special lighting effects and stage graphics offer a visual delight to the audience. Upon conclusion, all the dancers magically disappear into the fog, and the stage goes dark once again. The audience applauds enthusiastically. Alex reappears and introduces the New Washington event coordinator, who gives a brief speech.

"Our next performers are none other than the New Washington Philharmonic Orchestra, presenting a medley of classical music for your enjoyment," Alex says.

Once again, the stage goes dark. As the indigo floodlights softly illuminate the stage, the orchestra magically appears. Following their performance, Alex reappears under a spotlight, the rest of the stage remains dark.

"At this time, I would like to introduce Doctor Robert Riggin, chief science officer of the New Washington Research Institute," Alex says.

The audience applauds enthusiastically.

"Thank you, Alex," Robert begins, "and welcome, dignitaries and guests. The Dream Palladium is a culmination of the ingenuity and creative efforts of a team of outstanding individuals, ranging from the design team to the construction team, the hardware development team, the software development team, and the human biological engineering team. They overcame what were deemed to be insurmountable obstacles and achieved the impossible. Their efforts are documented in photos shown in a slideshow on the overhead monitors. Let us offer them a token of our appreciation."

Raucous cheers and enthusiastic applause take place.

"We should also recognize the contributions of our medical research team for developing the uplink port that enabled the new technology unveiled today to become a reality," Robert continues. "You have the unique privilege of being the first audience to be introduced to a new technology that offers a glimpse of the future."

As Robert pauses, a second Robert Riggin joins him on stage. The audience gasps.

"It's OK," Robert assures them. "Don't be alarmed. It's me times two. The person beside me, the dance troupe, and the orchestra are actually virtual mirror images of themselves and are not simply holographic entities, as one might assume. Other than myself, the real performers were not physically here, but their conscious state was, along with their physical mirror image. They truly believed they were on the Dream Palladium stage performing in front of an audience. This capability will have a huge impact on how we live going forward. You will be hearing a lot more about this new technology in the days to come. Now I'll turn the proceedings back over to Alex."

Robert and his mirror image vanish.

Following more applause, the stage and auditorium is darkened, and a single spotlight shines on Alex.

"Now we will proceed with the official grand opening and the ribbon-cutting ceremony," he announces.

The Dream Palladium's executive management team walks on stage to cut the ribbon. A mirrored in orchestra strikes up some lively music. The orchestra is physically located at an off-site location and is once again a virtual mirror image appearing on stage. Black, white, and blue graphics are displayed on a circular series of video screens located on the outer wall of the control room suspended over centre stage. As the orchestra entertains the guests, we leave the skybox, change into our sleepwear, and are ushered to a holding area next to the stage, ready to be introduced to the audience.

"And now it's time to introduce the dream team. Today we have two individuals and one family of dreamers to introduce. Let me present dreamer number one: Russell Fyfe, better known as "Rusty," comes to us from the New Los Angeles Correctional Institution where he is serving a five-year sentence. As a participant in the Dream Palladium grand opening, he has been offered a choice of rewards. Those include education credits, a one-year Dream Palladium credit to attend publicly offered events, or have one wish granted by the dreamer rewards committee at their discretion. He hopes to be granted one wish and use it to get out of prison to make a fresh start with a new life. Please welcome Rusty Fyfe."

Rusty waves to the audience as he walks over to stand next to Alex. The audience reacts favourably to Rusty's blue-and-white striped sleepwear and offers enthusiastic applause.

"Nice sleepwear," Alex says. "Rusty, are you looking forward to your experience?"

"I sure am. Beats the hell out of being in prison. Can I say hi to my mates?"

Alex nods. "Sure, go ahead."

"Hi, guys," Rusty says, looking into the camera. "T'was nice knowin' ya. I told you I'd get out of prison, and I'll soon be a free man!"

"You're sure your wish will be granted, are you?"

"You bet I am!"

Alex directs Rusty to make his way over to his assigned reclining chair, and he stands next to it.

"Next, we have Miss Kaylee Parker," Alex says, "a brilliant research scientist from the New Washington Research Institute. Kaylee, come on out!"

The audience applauds as I roll out on a power scooter in my lamb-patterned pink sleepwear, stopping next to Alex.

"Welcome, Kaylee. Great sleepwear. So, please tell us about your main area of focus at the institute."

"I'm currently working on ways for the human body to regenerate or repair damaged tissue to restore normal functionality."

"That sounds pretty interesting. Are you excited to be on the first ever Dream Palladium dream team?"

"I am. I was a little nervous before coming on stage. There are so many people, but I'm OK now."

Alex smiles. "Thank you, Kaylee, for joining us today. I hope you enjoy your dream experience. I'll ask you to please head over to your assigned reclining chair."

Alex turns back to the camera. "Our remaining members of today's dream team are the Hart family. They have come to us from New Los Angeles. Hart family, come on out."

Looking a little nervous, they walk onto the stage and join Alex.

"Here we have a family of four who will experience a family dream together. First, we have Ryan."

Ryan waves to the audience.

"Ryan is currently a project engineer for the Uplink Technologies Corporation. Next, we have Ryan's lovely wife, Melissa, who works at the New Los Angeles orthodontic clinic."

Melissa also waves to the audience.

"And next we have Jayden."

Jayden waves as well.

"Jayden is ten years old and has an adventurous spirit. Last but not least, we have Mia."

Mia waves, with some assistance from her mom.

"Eight years old with, as mom says, an independent personality all her own," Alex says.

The audience laughs.

Alex turns to Ryan. "So, are you and your family ready for your adventure today?"

"We are. We're a little anxious but really excited, right, guys?"

Melissa, Jayden, and Mia all nod in agreement.

"You'll be participating in a family dream where your dreams will join together as one," Alex explains. "Hart family, please proceed to your assigned reclining seats."

All six seats are located centre stage. They are set up in a circle with each dreamer's footrest facing the audience, and each seat is illuminated under a separate spotlight. The seats are black and smoothly contoured, similar to the audience seats, with a clear canopy in the open position that will enclose the occupants' head and chest. Each has an illuminated name plate below the footrest showing the dreamer's name. The perimeter of each seat back is illuminated with a thin blue-and-red band. The control panel on the end of each seat indicates some information for each dreamer with various coloured displays. We were informed at our orientation session that all dream activity and the dreamers' health status as well as the audience are managed by the Infinium computer system housed in an underground facility directly below the Dream Palladium.

"It's time," Alex says. "Dreamers, please be seated and prepare to embark on your journey."

As everyone else complies, I am also seated, with some assistance. A low-volume tone plays continuously throughout the auditorium. The auditorium lights remain dim while spotlights illuminate each of us, our excitement building.

"Audience, now that you have completed your dreamer selection, please sit back and relax while your canopies enclose you in your climate-controlled environment," Alex instructs. "Your tablet status bar should be green, signifying that you are good to go."

Our canopies slowly close.

As the overhead spotlights gradually dim and our canopies fully close, I feel a relaxing sensation throughout my body while I am being subjected to a dose of happy gas that will mentally stimulate me and enable my dream to begin.

"Let the dreams begin!" Alex announces.

OK, Kaylee, relax, I tell myself. *There's nothing to worry about. Just chill.*

Slipping into a deep sleep, I experience parallel dreams where in one, I am in the process of solving a complex mathematical equation by writing the mathematical formula on a purple digital chalkboard with a yellow marker, and in the other dream, I am playing dress-up as a princess in my castle, looking for my pink pony. I finish the math equation and instantly find myself in a magnificent ornate theatre filled with people. I'm playing classical music on a gold grand piano on a darkened stage with a bright spotlight shining down upon me. I'm dressed in a formal black sequin evening gown wearing a diamond tiara and am accompanied by an unseen orchestra. I play a variety of compositions and then suddenly find myself playing a harp solo. When the song ends, the audience offers generous applause. I close my eyes momentarily. When I open them again, I find myself in an orange lab coat in a dark chemistry lab. I'm standing at a brightly lit blue workbench pouring a green solution into a test tube half full of red fluid. A chemical reaction occurs where purple smoke fills the air, to the point where nothing can be seen. When the air finally clears, I am in my white sleepwear travelling through outer space approaching the outer rings of Saturn and discover that the rings consist of millions of tiny ice crystals shimmering like diamonds. Passing through the rings offers spectacular views of the rings and Saturn as well. I swing past Saturn and continue toward other planets in the Milky Way.

Meanwhile, in my parallel dream, I find my pink pony and ride it to a lush green meadow with lots of pretty flowers of every colour imaginable and see a multitude of animal-shaped bushes. I notice one that one looks like a huge elephant with big tusks. I stop at a nearby brook, and my pony drinks the purple water. Little white birds land on tree branches overhead, chirp at one another for a few seconds, and then suddenly fly away. Then my pony takes me to a merry-go-round in a meadow with a calliope playing horse-riding music. I climb onto the merry-go-round and then hop onto a large white horse with a gold saddle and a rainbow-coloured mane. I ride my horse around and around for the longest time. After that, I run through a meadow full of pretty little flowers and see black, white, and blue butterflies flitting about.

Back on my pink pony, I approach a pretty white house with blue windows, and I discover it is full of all sorts of dolls. I choose a baby doll to hold briefly and then put it in a small crib, and it falls asleep. All of the other dolls go to sleep too. When I leave the dollhouse bedroom, I open a door and see my mom in a yellow kitchen preparing cookie dough. My mom motions me to come and help her make some chocolate-chip cookies, so I begin to stir blue chocolate chips into the thick green cookie dough. We empty the dough onto a cookie sheet and drop more handfuls of orange chocolate chips onto the unbaked cookie dough that covers the baking sheet. Then we put the cookie sheet in the oven. The large cookie bakes instantly, and after removing it from the oven, we break our pan-sized cookie into large abstractly shaped chunks. We both enjoy sampling the yummy cookies.

I close my eyes again, and when my eyes open, I find myself in a pet store full of kittens and puppies. I sit on the floor, laughing as they all compete with one another, endlessly seeking my attention.

My dream is ending, and I begin to wake up. An assistant is right next to me looking down at me as I awaken, and we smile at one another. The overhead spotlights activate as our reclining chairs return to the upright position with our canopies open. I can't believe how happy I was to be free of the wheelchair in my dream, albeit for a brief time. It was so wonderful.

The audience is now wide awake, and their canopies have also retracted to the open position.

"Did everyone enjoy their dream adventure today?" Alex asks.

The audience offers enthusiastic applause along with a few cheers and whistles.

Alex turns toward the dreamers, who are standing beside their seats in their sleepwear—all of them except me, that is.

"Dreamers, please, come on over here and line up beside me," he says.

We all make our way over to Alex, with me taking a little longer as someone helps me onto my power scooter.

"Let's put our hands together and show these fine folks how much we appreciate their volunteering to participate in the Dream Palladium's grand opening," Alex says.

Once again, the audience offers passionate applause and cheers along with a standing ovation.

"All of the dreamers get to choose from three prize offerings," Alex continues. "Just to remind you, the first is to be granted educational credits or a one-year VIP pass to attend Dream Palladium events, and the third option is to be granted one wish that is within reason and is at the discretion of the dreamer rewards committee."

Alex turns to me. "So, Kaylee, tell me which prize option you're going to choose."

"I'll take the wish option. My wish is to receive approval to continue with tissue-regrowth research so that eventually my spinal cord can be fixed and I can walk. The most important goal for me right now is to be free of my wheelchair."

"Kaylee, we will do everything in our power to facilitate tissue-regrowth research that will hopefully make it possible to repair your spinal cord," Alex replies.

The audience cheers in support of my plans.

"Hart family," Alex continues, "what prize option do you choose?"

"We have agreed to opt for educational credits to put toward Jayden and Mia's education," Ryan says.

"Great!" Alex replies. "I'm sure the credits will be put to good use."

Alex looks at Rusty. "What are you going for?"

"Are you kiddin'? I'm choosing the wish option. My wish is to be a free man from this day forward with my criminal record wiped clean. I think that I damn well deserve a second chance."

"Our judges will give your wish full consideration, but I make no promises," Alex replies. "Dreamers, all of you except for Rusty are free to go and exit the same way you came on stage. Thanks to all of you for making the Dream Palladium's grand opening a huge success!"

The audience applauds one final time as the dreamers leave the stage, with the exception of Rusty.

"Thank you for coming to the Dream Palladium's grand opening, and we hope to see you again," Alex says to the audience. "Keep checking the event calendar for upcoming events."

Alex and Rusty remain on stage as Rusty nervously awaits the verdict. After a few minutes, a young lady comes on stage and hands Alex an envelope.

"May I have your attention please," Alex says, holding the envelope up. "I have the judge's response to Rusty's wish, and I'll read it aloud.

"'We, the judges of the Dream Palladium's grand opening have given due consideration of the request submitted by Russell Fyfe, and the panel's decision is to grant Russell Fyfe his wish with the provision that he must perform two hundred documented hours of community service.'" Alex turns to Rusty. "Russell, do you agree with these terms and conditions?"

"Yes! Yes! I agree! I'm the happiest man on the planet right now. Damn, I told my buddies I would get out of prison, and I did!"

"You will also receive some educational credits to help you start your new life," Alex adds.

He instructs Rusty to make his way back to the hospitality centre, where he will sign some paperwork and leave a free man.

CHAPTER 13

I meet up with Jess one day after work at our favourite café for supper and to relax for a while.

Jess arrives first, and I join her for a pre-supper beverage.

"Hey, how are you doing?" Jess asks.

"Wonderful," I reply. "I heard an acronym today that I have never heard before. Two men in lab coats were passing by in the opposite direction, and I clearly heard the term 'VE.' One of the men looked at me as they passed by, and I'm not sure why. Have you ever heard of anything like that?"

"No," Jess replies, "but I did find out from a friend that some sort of top-secret project is underway with super-tight security."

"Interesting," I reply. "We haven't expanded our lab facilities, so I don't know where the lab would be for this project."

"I think the lab isn't in this facility so as to maintain absolute secrecy," Jess says. "I have connections on the darknet that may have some info. Let me do some digging and see what I can find out."

"What's the darknet?" I ask. "Oh, never mind. I don't want to know. OK. I just might visit Robert and simply ask him what the acronym means."

"No, don't do that," Jess says. "He might have you locked up in a prison cell! Just chill until we meet again."

"OK."

The next day, I am summoned to report immediately to Robert's office and I'm not sure if I should inquire about the term VE or if that might get me into serious trouble. While on route to Robert's office, I am still unsure about mentioning the term "VE" to him. As soon as I arrive at his outer office, his secretary ushers me directly into his office, where he is reading something on his computer monitor. He looks over at me and smiles. I have a ginormous lump in my throat at the thought of asking about VE and fear his reaction.

"Kaylee, hi. I'm so glad to see you," Robert exclaims.

I look up sheepishly and then begin to relax a little. Recalling the man in the lab coat staring at me, thankfully, there are no armed guards at the doorway behind me, ready to take me away.

"Hello. You wanted to see me?"

"Yes," Robert replies. "We're continuing to develop a top-secret project that was started way before the firestorm occurred. I can't divulge too many details, but I can tell you that your skill set would be of great benefit to expedite the project, as time is of the essence." He pauses for a few seconds to allow me to process the information. "What I am asking is, would you be interested in joining an elite off-site research team from now until the project is complete?"

My brain is in overdrive. I breathe a huge sigh of relief. I thought that one of the men in lab coats reported me and that I was in serious trouble.

"Yes, I absolutely would. This wouldn't have anything to do with VE by chance, would it?"

"Where did you hear that term?" Robert asks, his face reddening. "No one outside of me and two other people in this city know anything about VE."

I have never seen Robert so angry, and now I'm scared.

"I overheard two people wearing white lab coats mention the term as they passed by me in the hallway," I venture.

Robert frowns. "Since you know about VE, you have become a security risk and are to be transported to the off-site lab immediately. Your belongings will be delivered to you, and you'll have no outside contact with anyone from here on in."

I am on the verge of tears. I know I hit a nerve and wonder why there's a need for such secrecy. What is this project about?

Seconds later, Robert recovers his composure and returns to his soft-spoken self. "I'm sorry for being so harsh. You know, you could be a great spy. I can share that the term VE stands for 'Virtual Earth.' I'll let you think about that for a while. However, I can't allow any details of 'VE' to leak out to the general population."

Two security guards appear at Robert's office and escort me down some darkened hallways that are off limits to the general population and then through a warehouse full of plastic-wrapped skids over to a small waiting room adjacent to the hovercopter air transport apron. One of the dock attendants enters the waiting room.

"Are you Kaylee Parker?" he asks abruptly.

"Yes, I am."

"Please hold up your security bracelet. I need to verify your identity."

I comply, and he scans my bracelet. Then he hands me my carry-on bag and departs. It contains two photos and my whale plus some clothing and toiletries.

It feels like I'm being sent to some sort of detention centre.

"If you have to use the facilities, do it now. If not, please follow me."

"No, I'm fine," I reply, shaking my head.

He hands me an oxy-pack to put on. Then we depart the office building and enter the warehouse, once again navigating our way around various skids of materials ready for shipment, presumably to the off-site lab.

Departing the warehouse, we approach a waiting aircraft where I am assisted up a loading ramp into the hovercopter's cargo hold. I realize I am the only passenger. For safety reasons, my wheelchair is clamped securely in place, and a tie-down strap secures me to my wheelchair. There are no windows or easily accessed seats, so I have to stay in my wheelchair for the duration. That's OK, as I'll probably sleep most of the way.

The hovercopter pilot pokes her head into the cargo hold. "Welcome aboard. I'm Tracy Newbury, your pilot. Sorry, there are no in-flight videos or snacks. But I can offer you a flask of water and a couple of pillows from the first-aid cabinet.

"Thank you. I've never flown in a hovercopter before, so I hope I won't be airsick."

"Here, if you feel like you're going to be sick, use this bag," Tracy says, handing one to me. "The rule in my ship is if you make a mess, you clean it up, so please use the bag."

As the cargo bay door closes, the copter shudders briefly as the rotors rev to full throttle and then reduce to warm up the nuclear ion engines. The rotors rev again, and liftoff is so smooth, I can hardly tell we're in the air. I feel like I'm in a tomb with no windows. After a few sips of water, I rest my head on the pillows, leaning against a crate. Sleep comes quickly. The flight is smooth and my sleep continues uninterrupted until I hear the rotor speed change. Splashing a little water on my face helps to wake me up as we approach our destination. Tracy pokes her head back into the cargo bay.

"Hey there. Are you awake?"

"Barely, but yes, I am."

"Five minutes to touchdown. And don't be surprised if it's cold and damp when we deplane."

The rotor sound becomes extremely loud, like we're in some sort of enclosure, and then it subsides to the point where it can't be heard.

"Welcome to your new home!" Tracy says, returning. "You'll have to put on an oxy-pack."

"Where are we?"

"Can't tell you," Tracy replies. "Besides, this place has no name."

She helps me deplane and then we proceed through an airlock into a huge enclosed hangar bay where the air is breathable. I remove my oxy-pack and see a man rapidly approaching.

"Hi, Kaylee. My name is Earl Houseman, and I'm the base commander here at this fine facility. Please follow me."

We leave the hangar and head toward the staff quarters. My new home consists of a small sitting room with a chair and lamp, a bedroom, and a tiny bathroom that is not wheelchair friendly.

"We will remove the partitions between your sitting room, bedroom, and bathroom to make it easier for you to get around," Earl says.

"Thank you," I reply, nodding.

Two maintenance men arrive. They finish the job in thirty minutes and then leave. I don't even get a chance to thank them, and I suspect there was to be no conversation due to the tight security environment I am in.

CHAPTER 14

Thomas Williams and Robert Riggin, who have known one another for a number of years, meet face to face in the presidential oval office with Thomas sitting at his desk. Thomas is a short, round man in his fifties, who is almost completely bald with an oval face and a moustache. Robert is escorted into the oval office, and they greet one another.

"Welcome, Robert," Thomas says. "Please be seated. I need you to update me on the status of Project Utopia. I've been following your monthly updates, and I'm anxious to know the state of readiness and whether we're in a position to use this new technology, if needed. We're having increasing reliability issues with the oxygen enhancement equipment both here and in New Los Angeles."

Robert nods. "At present, if New Washington and New Los Angeles should suffer an environmental catastrophe, we're in a position to quickly complete Project Utopia or Virtual Earth to enable humankind to be able to exist in a virtual environment. Of course, the leadership councils of New Washington and New Los Angeles would have to endorse this action and authorize more resources to further shorten the timeline for VE to be fully operational."

"Will our day-to-day routine be emulated, or will our virtual living situation be different?" Thomas asks.

"Virtual Earth is capable of emulating life in our domed cities, replicating the way we live down to the finest detail."

"How quickly can Virtual Earth be ready?"

"With sufficient resources, we can be in a position to expedite completion of Virtual Earth. The structure is ninety-nine percent complete, and the software platform is in the testing and evaluation phase," Robert explains. "The Dream Palladium's grand opening played a critical role in the validation of the Virtual Earth operating platform, giving us confidence that we're ready to deploy it, if needed."

"So, you're saying we could migrate over to Virtual Earth now if we had to do so? Robert, please tell me what I need to hear."

"Possibly in two weeks, yes. A few finishing touches remain to be completed. Barring any software validation issues, we can be ready that quickly."

Thomas nods. "Good. I'll call an emergency Leadership Council meeting to gain buy-in to the prospect of our being forced to live in Virtual Earth if an environmental catastrophe should occur."

The following morning, Thomas and Robert meet with Harper Jackson, who is New Washington's chief medical officer, Vivian Dwight, who is New Los Angeles's chief medical officer, Forrest Cameron, New Los Angeles's chief environmental officer, and Marek Zielinski, New Washington's chief environmental officer, to discuss Virtual Earth.

"I have an important topic that we urgently need to discuss," Thomas says, opening the meeting. "Members of the NLA Leadership Council are on a video conference call with us as well. Robert will fill us in on the situation."

"Thank you, Mr. President," Robert begins. "We depend heavily on our life-support systems to maintain a comfortable living environment. The problem is that we do not have a back-up or alternative technology if a catastrophic environmental life-support system failure occurs. Living in the outside world is not an option, and that places our population at risk."

"We have managed so far," Harper says. "Why the sense of urgency?"

"Right now, our life-support systems are functioning, but they could fail, so we're trying to be proactive. We have resumed working on Project Utopia, also known as Virtual Earth, which could potentially offer us a safe refuge that will enable us to go on with our lives in a protected and secure virtual environment."

"What?" Harper exclaims. "Surely, you're not suggesting this as a back-up if our living environment is compromised. How can we even consider this as a failsafe? Plus, we can't even consider this course of action without buy-in from the general population. They need to agree to exist in this Virtual Earth you're proposing. We need their consent!"

All the Leadership Council members are shocked and horrified with the concept of the population essentially dying and redefining what it means to be alive.

"I agree," Vivian says. "There's an ethical value to consider here. It's called freedom of choice. We have an obligation to offer the general population the choice to migrate or not."

"Both of you are correct," Thomas says, "and in keeping with such freedoms, there should be an open examination of the facts. We need to take sufficient time to deliberate the pros and cons of migrating to Virtual Earth."

"That all sounds well and good," Robert interjects, "but there are two small problems. First, we simply may not have time for endless discussions about the ethics and logistics of the migration if an emergency situation should occur. Second, a violent clash between those in agreement and those who are against migrating could occur."

"What if an emergency situation suddenly arises?" Forrest asks, sounding frustrated. "If the life-support systems fail before a majority of the population is convinced VE is the right option for survival, there are no other options currently available. At that point in time debating the ethics and logistics of migrating to live in a virtual world is futile. Right now, we should be focusing on how we can safely move the population over to Virtual Earth."

"Forrest is right," Robert says. "We must be prepared to initiate the migration over to Virtual Earth on short notice. Thomas will ultimately make the decision based upon our giving him the authority to do so. I think we should vote to endorse this action."

"I do not feel at all comfortable with this plan," Marek says. "I vote no."

A show of hands takes place, and the leadership council members vote not to endorse the proposition to migrate over to Virtual Earth if a crisis should arise.

"I think it would be prudent at this time to recommend that the Leadership Council members join me for a tour of our off-site research lab and Virtual Earth to gain a better understanding of this proposal," Robert says.

"I propose that the Virtual Earth project be put on hold until we make our final decision to approve or disapprove continuing," Harper demands.

The Leadership Council members vote in favour of the proposal.

"The project will be put on hold," Thomas says. "Leadership Council members, do you agree with Robert's recommendation? Let's have a show of hands."

Everyone is in agreement.

"It's settled then. Robert, please arrange for the tour to take place as soon as possible. As for the rest of you, please keep in mind that our discussion today must be considered highly confidential, and all matters herein are to be held in the strictest of confidence. The meeting is adjourned."

CHAPTER 15

A remote hidden underground bunker formerly used to store naval supplies and located 180 miles northwest of New Washington now houses a group of survivors. Juan Garcia, the self-appointed leader of his band of followers, is standing on an elevated platform in a dimly lit underground chamber. A stiff-mannered man, he is forty-two years old, has a full beard and is a little overweight. He is wearing khaki shorts and a desert-tan short-sleeved shirt with many pockets. Prior to the firestorm event, he was a member of a radical group of extremists who believed that any government, past or present, is full of crooked politicians who are trying to undermine democracy for their own gain.

He is standing in front of a large hand-drawn map of the New Washington to New Los Angeles corridor. He is preparing to address an audience composed of twenty-four men and women who survived the firestorm and have formed an alliance. He believes they are considered undesirable human capital, and for that reason, they were denied entry into New Washington.

Juan brings the meeting to order. "We have learned that the Research Institute in New Washington is working on a major project, and it is nearing completion. We have also learned that it will act as a fail-safe backup if their infrastructure experiences a catastrophic failure and is no longer capable of supporting human life."

The audience erupts with murmurs in response to the news.

"Also, we know that we will not be able to stay here forever, putting our existence at risk. The plan going forward is to eliminate the populations of both cities and then occupy the NW food-production facility, which has its own life-support systems. We must act now to prevent them from bringing this mysterious project to completion."

Once again, the audience members talk amongst themselves as Juan takes a sip of water.

"I want to introduce you to our newest member of the Freedom Alliance. Jess, stand up, so everyone can see you."

The audience welcomes Jess with applause and verbal greetings. Jess waves and then sits down.

"Jess has come to us from New Washington. She told me that she learned of the name of the project, referred to by the initials 'VE,' from a friend. We need to find out what that term refers to. To do so, we need to send a recon team to infiltrate New Washington, find the weaknesses in their life-support system, and then develop a strategy to capitalize on them. Jess will guide the recon team."

After the meeting, Juan meets with Jess and Martina to discuss the plan of action. Martina is tall and slender with a very rugged no-nonsense demeanour. She has had special ops training and has been involved in various recon missions. The pair of them will form the recon team.

"Jess, what do you suggest?" Juan asks.

"We can enter New Washington through the food-production facility. I know the layout, and a security bypass is already in place there. Once inside, we can use the computer terminal there to obtain information on their life-support systems."

"What about security?" Martina asks. "Are there cameras?"

"At night, there are no security patrols, and security is limited to drones," Jess replies. "Cameras don't work because they keep fogging up in the moist environment."

The following night, outfitted in black, the recon team enters the food-production facility via the roll-up door at the loading dock. After ensuring that no drones are in sight, they make their way to a nearby computer terminal. Martina hacks into the maintenance server and copies various files onto her memory module while Jess stands watch. Martina also tries to hack into the Research Institute server to see if there is anything there pertaining to VE but is unsuccessful. As Martina completes her task, they see a security drone approaching.

"Get down and don't move!" Jess whispers.

They both drop to their knees and remain motionless as the drone stops momentarily above them and then continues on.

"Let's get out of here!" Martina says.

"Follow me," Jess says.

They exit the building and return to their base. Juan and Martina examine the files to assess weaknesses and determine targets to attack where the likelihood of success is high.

Afterwards, Juan meets with Jess, Martina, and Brad.

"After studying their infrastructure files, it's clear that their weakness is their oxygen-enhancement system, which is used to maintain a breathable environment. The key components affecting oxygen enhancement are the manufacture of spare parts for the cooling system compressors and their ability to produce refrigerant for the cooling towers."

"We also confirmed that the food-production facility operates independently with its own life-support system," Martina says. "It will meet our needs perfectly."

"It's imperative that we attack the oxygen-enhancement facilities in New Washington and New Los Angeles simultaneously to cripple their ability to maintain a breathable environment," Juan says. "The populations of both cities will then be forced to evacuate the domed cities. Mass panic will prevail, and most of the population will not survive."

"But why must the populations of both cities have to suffer and die? It just seems so wrong," Jess asks.

Juan states, "I'll tell you why. My pregnant wife was trapped in our house under debris resulting from the firestorm, and when we found her, she was very weak and had breathing issues. She died a week after we rescued her. If we had been allowed entry into the rescue shelter, I believe that they could have saved her life. Now it will be their turn to suffer as my wife did."

"I'm so sorry that your wife and baby died," Jess offers. "But your plan of action still seems extreme."

"It isn't, as far as I am concerned. End of discussion," Juan says in a terse tone of voice.

Juan calls another meeting to outline the proposed course of action. Everyone votes in favour of attacking the New Washington and New Los Angeles oxygen-enhancement systems.

CHAPTER 16

First thing the next morning, Earl escorts me to the lab and introduces me to the staff, which includes four computer programmers and three biological research engineers. One person of note is Stanley. He is a paraplegic in his fifties. He is seated in his power scooter at his computer terminal and speaks by typing text, which is translated electronically into speech. He and I make a connection seeing as both of us have physical limitations, and we have many conversations with one another. He tells me he is angry with the government for how he was mistreated throughout his life. He said that, as a child, the government wanted him placed in an institution. While growing up, every time he wanted to further his education, he was denied due to his disability. He said if it weren't for his caregiver's persistence, he would not have become a computer programmer.

"Seems like we're outcasts from civilization, doesn't it?" Stanley says.

"Yes," I agree. "We're so isolated here, with no contact with the outside world."

"That's not entirely true," Stanley replies. "Officially, you're correct, but I've reconfigured some server nodes to covertly allow me to contact a couple of my friends in New Washington."

"Oh. I wonder if you could send my friend Jess Spencer a message telling her that I'm OK and that I miss her."

"Sure," Stanley replies. "I can have my friend in New Washington relay your message."

At that moment, Stuart, a biological engineer, approaches Stanley's workstation. He is a stalwart Scotsman with the accent to prove it.

"OK, Kaylee, are you ready to enter our miniature version of Virtual Earth?" Stuart asks.

"Sure," I reply. "As long as I'm not going to be stranded there forever!"

Everyone laughs as I follow Stuart over to the transfer hub and prepare to migrate to VE.

"Today while you're in VE, you'll be participating in a sensory test," Stuart explains. "We need to assess whether different test subjects experience the same sensory inputs in differing situations. Your body will remain in the transfer hub chair, but your mind will be in VE."

"You mean, it's like being a dreamer at the Dream Palladium?" I ask.

"Yes, exactly," Stuart replies, nodding. "In fact, most of the Dream Palladium software was developed here, as the software applications are quite similar. Are you ready?"

I am assisted from my wheelchair into a comfortable reclining chair. A communication harness is attached to my uplink port. A transparent mask with a clear plastic tube attached is positioned over my face, and I immediately smell a pleasant flowery scent.

"Don't worry," Stuart assures me. "The face mask is to administer a small dose of happy gas, which will assist with the transition into VE."

I close my eyes for a few seconds. When I open them, the first thing I see is a beautiful park-like promenade with meandering walkways bordered with colourful flowerbeds and shade trees everywhere. And I can walk! Just like in my dream at the Dream Palladium.

"How do you feel?" Stuart asks.

"Wonderful!" I reply. "I can walk!"

"That's great. We purposely removed your disability from your profile, so you can enjoy not being in a wheelchair for a while. You obviously approve. So then, let's go through the sensory checklist and see how you're doing. Are you comfortable in the environment? Not too hot or too cold?"

"The temperature is perfect, and the humidity level is fine too," I reply.

"That's great. Please describe what you see, hear, and smell."

"The sky is a perfect shade of sky blue, and the promenade is visually stunning as I slowly navigate the walkways. The flowers have a pleasing fragrance, and the trees offer shade from the warmth of the sunlight. Birds are chirping too."

"That's great. Next, we want to have a look at your sense of touch and taste. If you continue down the walkway, you'll see that a patio is set up with a table and chairs. You can have lunch there. Please describe your experience to us."

I seat myself and survey the wonderful array of lunch options set before me. "The cloth napkin I am unfolding and placing on my lap has a slightly rough texture and is somewhat stiff to open, as expected. The serving tongs are plastic and feel smooth and comfortable to use. I'm using the tongs to serve myself fresh garden vegetables, and everything seems quite normal. Now I'm sampling a ham sandwich with lettuce and mayonnaise, which tastes amazing. All of the food samples taste perfect, as is their texture. Everything is just like in the real world."

"Terrific," Stuart replies. "Please tell me about your sense of touch."

"Everything so far seems normal. I rinsed my fingers in the lemony water in the finger bowl, and I could sense that the water is cool to the touch. The water splashed and dripped from my fingers as I would expect it to."

"OK, good. Well, that's it for the sensory test," Stuart says. "It's time to leave VE."

"I wish I could stay here forever," I reply. "It's so wonderful to be able to walk."

Everything goes dark, and when I open my eyes, I see Stuart looking at me as he removes the face mask and communication cable.

"How are you feeling now?" he asks.

"Fine. I feel refreshed like I just had a nap."

Stuart smiles. "Good. Thanks for taking the sensory test."

"You're welcome."

After I get back into my wheelchair, Stanley turns in his power chair to face me.

"Come here," his tablet says.

I wheel over to him, and he shows me more text on his tablet: "There is no Jess Spencer listed in the New Washington database."

I am in a state of shock. Did she escape from NW? Was she thrown into a prison cell because she knew about VE?

I thank Stanley for his help and then head back to my room.

At the end of the next workday, Stanley pulls me aside. "I have recently made contact with a rebel group known as the Freedom Alliance. They asked if I knew of a top-secret project nearing completion and asked for my help to come up with a way to sabotage it. I haven't responded to their request yet."

"Right now, I'm not happy with the powers that be either," I admit. "I was forced out of New Washington, because when I asked what VE meant, they thought I was a security risk."

Most of my work at the off-site lab is to ensure that the delicate electro-chemical balance and its linkage to a series of complex emotional parameters transitions over to VE for each person along with their physical DNA-related attributes. That data has been accumulated from test subjects and their experiences in VE, focusing on their feelings and emotions under varying conditions. One of the concerns with living in VE is to determine if people can still fall in love and another is the human conscience in relation to acts of violence.

I forward my report to Robert, and he indicates that I can return to New Washington in a few days to continue my research there. The following day Robert messages me.

"Hi, Kaylee. I know that you're feeling sad about the project cancellations. The Leadership Council members are strongly opposed to using VE as a back-up if our life-supporting systems should fail. I'm on my way to the Research Institute lab with the Leadership Council. We plan to tour the off-site lab and Virtual Earth, and I'm hoping that you can remain at the off-site base and join me to be a tour guide."

I hesitate for a few seconds and realize that my words might sway the opinion of some council members so they will change their perception and endorse the project.

"Yes. I'm willing to be a guide."

"Great. We'll meet in the boardroom at 1:00 p.m. today and depart immediately."

The tour attendees include Robert, chief environment officers Marek Zielinski of New Washington and Forrest Cameron of New Los Angeles, and chief medical officers Harper Jackson of New Washington and Vivian Dwight of New Los Angeles.

On route to the off-site research facility, with heavy clouds overhead, they fly at a low altitude, skimming over ice-cold steel-blue water, with sheer rock faces on either side of the narrow channel. They descend even lower while reducing their airspeed and see a brightly lit horizontal opening in the rock face up ahead. The aircraft eases itself above the landing platform and then sets down. A mothballed nuclear sub is tied up to their left in the submarine pen. As the hovercopter powers down, the crew and visitors are welcomed by Earl Houseman, the base commander, and then follow him into the facility.

"Welcome, everyone," Earl says. "My name is Earl Houseman and I am the base commander of this facility. Please follow me."

Earl is a career military man in his fifties. He has been in charge of the facility since it opened and considers the base to be his home.

A large, well-lit service bay comes into view where a transport aircraft is being serviced. Distant voices echo off the rock walls as the technicians discuss their work. After departing the service bay, they're escorted to their rooms and given some time to freshen up.

At 1:00 p.m., we gather in a secure meeting room. Robert brings the meeting to order. "Earl Houseman will accompany us on part of the lab tour. He has something special to show you. I would also like to introduce you to Kaylee Parker. She is here on loan from the New Washington Research Institute and has just completed her work assignment. She will accompany us today to assist me with answering any questions you may have. Hopefully, your tour today will convince you that if our life-support systems fail, Virtual Earth would provide a safe refuge for the populations of both cities. Keep in mind that with the outside environment remaining contaminated for an unknown duration, there are few options available in the event of a catastrophic life-support system failure."

"It's going to take some convincing to make me change my mind and endorse this project," Harper says.

"Now, Harper, please keep an open mind today as we learn more about VE," Forrest urges.

"If there are no further questions, I suggest we start our tour," Robert says. "Earl, please lead the way."

As we proceed in single file down a long, narrow hallway, we pass by the crew quarters, a library, a video game/movie room, and a music-listening room. We also pass various offices and meeting rooms.

At the end of the hallway, an oversized door brings us into a lush tropical garden. The air is sweet with the scent of tropical plants and flowers. As we walk along a meandering pathway made of interlocking stones, brightly adorned butterflies dart about. I hear running water in the distance that sounds like a waterfall.

The pathway takes us to a circular patio with ergonomically shaped chairs placed in a circle facing the centre of the patio. Other seating is scattered throughout the garden as well. Behind us, water tumbles over an irregular rock face into a pond populated with aquatic plants where small orange-and-black striped fish swim lazily about.

"Isn't this something?" Earl asks. "This is my pride and joy, a place where everyone can come to relax after a hard day at the office. I think it's important that we connect with nature to maintain our mental well-being. All of the rest areas also offer happy gas, if desired, to enhance the relaxation experience."

"You've created an exceptional artificial environment here," Marek says. "I'm impressed."

"Thank you, Marek," Earl replies, smiling. "I've had an interest in horticulture for years, and now I can put my knowledge into practice. Oh, by the way, don't be alarmed, but if you look closely at the banyan tree to our right, you can see a large Burmese python resting on her favourite bough with her tail drooping. Fear not. She's harmless. She's been behaviourally modified with an uplink port and is not in any way a threat to our safety. Her name is Ula."

With that, Earl takes his leave. After a brief rest, we leave the garden and head over to the engineering lab complex. Upon entry to the visitor observation balcony, we see a brightly lit open-concept work area with desks placed in an unstructured, abstract pattern with test equipment and computer terminals scattered throughout the facility. Engineers and technicians are going about their tasks and interacting with one another or working quietly at their desks. In the far corner, a transfer hub sits unattended, and a shortened version of a memory pillar is glowing white with technicians gathered at a nearby control panel, watching the view screen.

"The brightly lit memory pillar over in the far corner of the lab contains a virtual representation of a real living environment that mimics a small sample of the real world down to the finest detail," Robert explains.

The elevated visitor balcony is isolated from the lab to allow the lab to continue with its activities uninterrupted.

"As you can see," Robert says, "the lab is a very busy place with verification testing of the Virtual Earth software platform in progress. They work long days to make sure that, in the event of our migration over to Virtual Earth, life thereafter will be flawless."

"So, right now they're simulating some people living in VE?" Vivian asks.

"Yes, and I've volunteered to be a test subject as well to assist with some of the testing," I say.

Harper turns to me. "How did you feel? What did it look like?"

"It was wonderful. The air was pure, and I could walk! I wanted to stay there forever."

Forrest smiles. "You've given VE a fine endorsement."

Robert explains that right now, they are mirroring in a few selected people from New Washington to beta test the VE hardware and software. The test subjects are living virtually in their replicated real-world environment in the memory pillar and are consciously reacting to the same stimuli as their counterparts in the real world. The technicians and engineers can use the transfer hub to invisibly witness the test subjects going about their daily business inside the system.

"Such an incredible evolution of technology to be able to live virtually for an indefinite period of time," Vivian remarks.

"Yes, and fortunately, we're in a position to transition over if needed," Robert says.

As we exit the visitor balcony to return to our quarters, we're confronted by a full-grown Bengal tiger sauntering down the hallway toward us. It approaches our group and stops beside Robert. He bends down so he can look directly at the tiger.

"Amy, I'm so glad to see you," Robert says.

He kneels down, hugs her, then pets her, and she starts to purr.

"Nice kitty," Harper says. "I hope you're not hungry!"

"Don't worry," Robert replies. "She's my girlfriend, and rest assured, she will not eat you! Her name is Amica, which is Latin for 'friend.' I call her Amy. If you look at her neck, you'll see that she's been fitted with an uplink port. She was part of a series of early government experiments in modified behavioural control using a computer interface. As such, her behaviour emulates that of an affectionate domestic cat."

"Yes, I can hear her purring just like my cat at home," Forrest says.

"The only food she recognizes are the sausages she gets twice per day," Robert explains. "She adores me and often sleeps in my room on her own large cat bed. Sometimes I take her outside on the flight deck to run and play, and we have a great time."

After our surprise encounter, we return to our rooms and relax until supper.

We meet the next morning in the conference room.

"Welcome, everyone. Today on our tour, you will see that we have built a safe sanctuary for the populations of New Washington and New Los Angeles. This project was started some time ago and we have embraced the latest technologies to complete this masterpiece of engineering.

"The on-site team here is very busy with their workload, so Kaylee will be joining us today," Robert announces. "Let's head over to the transfer hub."

Robert leads us through the crew quarters and down a long ramp. Then we traverse a series of underground passageways that take us to the transfer hub. Upon arrival, we enter a spacious, circular, softly lit room with an open centre area and enclosures with sliding glass doors placed around the perimeter. Each enclosure has a high-backed, padded reclining chair and a raised clear canopy. A green status light is illuminated above each enclosure door.

"We're about to transfer to VE," Robert explains. "Your conscious state will transfer while your physical bodies remain here for the duration of the visit. Upon your return, you'll awaken here."

"So, you mean to say that our minds will separate from our bodies?" Harper asks.

"Yes, that is correct," Robert replies. "You will be mirrored over to the VE site, which, by the way, is at the North Pole. VE had to be located there for reasons that will be explained during our tour.

"The transparent canopies will close when you are ready to transfer to Virtual Earth. When you are ready to transfer, press the green button on the armrest of your chair, and a small dose of happy gas will be administered as a part of the process to move your conscious state from here over to VE. So, please take a seat and make yourselves comfortable. I'll see you in a few minutes."

In a short time, we find ourselves in a transfer hub identical to the one we just departed from, except for the room is now a pale blue instead of a haze grey. We all gather in the open area of the transfer hub and look at one another, noting that we look the same as before. None of us can believe that we're actually there as we scope out our new surroundings.

"Welcome to Project Utopia," Robert says. "Everyone doing OK? Follow me, and we will visit the central VE control podium."

"Kaylee, you're not in your wheelchair!" Vivian exclaims. "How can that be?"

"That's right. My spinal cord defect was left out of my mirror profile, so I can walk."

"This technology is truly amazing!" Forrest says.

After entering the control room and ascending a stairway onto a perforated floor, we find ourselves standing in the middle of a dimly lit dome-like structure with view screens covering the ceiling and a dozen tall, monolithic computer towers on a raised illuminated floor. A black sphere is suspended from the ceiling overhead. It uses various colours of laser light to interact with the towers to manage various VE operating parameters. We can feel the cool air required to cool the towers passing over us.

Robert explains, "This is where we monitor and control all aspects of Virtual Earth. The black sphere receives information from numerous sources throughout VE and responds accordingly, issuing commands to the control nodes. Once VE is up and running smoothly, there will be little activity here and most of the control towers will go into sleep mode.

"Another feature of the control centre is to our left," Robert says. "Follow me, and we will visit our security and self-defence pods."

We walk a short distance and enter a separate softly lit dome with three large, curved wall-mounted monitors.

Robert continues, "Here we monitor all external activity for quite some distance and react to any suspected security breaches. Security data is forwarded to our VE security centre and monitored twenty-four/seven. We have weaponry in place to deal with any situation. Oh, and just so you know, we can differentiate between a real threat and a polar bear wandering by."

"So, security is fully automated," Forrest says, "What happens if a security breach is detected?"

"The VE chief security officer will be notified immediately and will determine what possible courses of action to consider." Robert shares. "If the situation poses a threat, the chief security officer will notify the president and await authorization to proceed with any countermeasures deemed necessary."

Marek nods in satisfaction. "It appears that VE is well protected."

"Yes, even though the site is isolated, safety is our top priority," Robert replies.

We retrace our steps, exiting the security centre and enter another pod.

Robert explains, "We need to ensure that the VE power supply is operating properly at all times and is well regulated. A geo-stationary satellite with a large solar panel array is positioned about 800 miles directly overhead to feed our ground power inlet with multiple continuous beams of energy. That is why VE is located at the North Pole. This provides enough power to operate VE with power to spare. We convert the solar energy into electrical power and charge our solid-state power bank continuously. VE operates at sixty percent capacity, and the system is virtually maintenance free. Under normal conditions, none of the VE control systems requires human intervention.

"Next, we'll make our way to the viewing platform inside the VE sphere," Robert adds.

We follow Robert, which takes us to an elevator, where we descend to the facility's lowest level. Then we navigate a dimly lit concrete corridor and enter an open area, stopping in front of a series of elevator doors. The left and right elevators show a red status, with the middle elevator showing green. The middle elevator door opens, and we file into the spacious car. We ascend briefly and then stop at the viewing platform level.

Stepping out of the elevator, we take in the immensity of the spherical structure that surrounds us. The coating on the inside of the sphere is an opaque off-white colour with a shiny surface that almost appears to be wet. Workmen, wearing bright orange reflective vests, are on an upper-level catwalk next to a series of folded mechanical arms. The arms and the catwalk are attached to a black circular vertical structure centrally positioned extending upward from the floor of the sphere. The mechanical arms are capable of accessing any surface location within the sphere.

Robert describes, "The coating that you see on the interior of the sphere is sprayed on using nozzles attached to mechanical arms. A workman is housed in the cab attached to the arm next to the nozzle to control the application of the heated liquid plasma. Once applied, the plasma cools and solidifies. The plasma is a newly developed technology and is made up of a fluid containing millions of microprocessors and router nodes. The coating is highly conductive and can move each packet of data at the speed of light, giving us infinite computing capacity. When operating, a lot of heat is given off and the plasma softens slightly, increasing its computing efficiency."

Just as Robert finishes, amber warning lights begin to flash and alarms sound.

Robert announces, "I have to leave you for a few minutes to take an important call. Kaylee will be in charge until I return."

"Listen up, everyone. I am going to play a recorded explanation of the plasma density test we will witness," I announce.

In Robert's absence, I find and play a recording that explains the plasma coating density test: "The plasma-application engineers are about to run a test sequence to verify the density of the plasma coating, which is so critical to the efficient movement of data. Any density variance can result in a hot spot and potentially cause an overload. Also, the plasma could experience a meltdown and burst into flames, possibly destroying Virtual Earth."

A heavily tinted shield drops down to cover the visitor viewing window, and the workmen vacate the sphere. As the cooling system ramps up, air movement causes a loud roaring sound to fill the sphere. Next, a low-frequency hum begins as the power supply is activated to power up the plasma coating. At first, nothing happens, but after a few seconds, the plasma begins to glow at floor level. Soon the plasma shines brilliantly from the floor to the highest point on the sphere. Initially, it's deep blue with some purple waves moving across the plasma. Then it changes gradually to a mixture of yellow and orange. After a few seconds the surface turns bright white with a few small, irregularly shaped grey patches. The test ends, and the tinted shield covering the visitor platform retracts. The sphere also goes silent.

"You've just witnessed a plasma coating density test," I explain. "I hope it wasn't too scary."

Robert's recording continues: "When operating, the plasma runs at a high temperature and requires a massive amount of airflow to keep things cool. The grey areas you observed on the dome's inner surface are what we call thin spots and need to have more plasma applied. Soon, the touch-ups will be complete, and the mechanical arms will be removed to make room for plasma memory pillars, which will fill the sphere. Right now, they are below the sphere's temporary floor and can be viewed after we exit the sphere."

Following Robert's recorded instructions, we take the same elevator down to where we began, and everyone follows me at a short distance to an open area with large tinted viewing windows. Beyond the windows, everything is dark. After locating a wall-mounted view screen adjacent to the windows, I follow Robert's instructions and enter a sequence on a keypad. Moments later, we're surprised to see a seemingly endless number of memory pillars come to life. They are tall and cylindrical with shallow spiraling flutes on their exterior. They go through a series of colour changes similar to the sequence we observed in the sphere during the power-up stage, but this time when finished, they remain at a deep indigo blue.

I play Robert's next recording: "We have twenty-one memory pillars in total, and the colouration you see now indicates that the pillars are in an idle state with no data movement occurring. When we run a data-flow test, watch and see what happens."

Following Robert's instructions, I run a short data-flow sequence, and the pillars change momentarily to a bright yellow colour. Then the test sequence ramps the data flow in each pillar up to maximum. The colour changes from blue to yellow with orange waves to red with white waves and then the red gradually disappears, leaving pure white light. The test shuts down, and the pillars return to a deep blue colour before powering down.

Robert re-joins us.

Robert says, "Thank you, Kaylee for your assistance. The pillars contain all of the human DNA, human memory data, and the current conscious state for the entire population of New Washington and New Los Angeles. Once the plasma coating is complete, the top of the pillars will be elevated and bonded to the sphere's plasma coating. When fully operational, data moves instantaneously to and from the pillars, interacting with the plasma coating on the sphere as people go about their daily business. The memory pillars consist of millions of microprocessors, routers, and memory nodes and continuously archive all human activity for each resident. That includes everything they say, see, do, and think as well as all sensory inputs. It also tracks everyone's movements. People's physical and mental health statuses are constantly monitored as well. You could say that the sphere represents our world as we know it today with some enhancements. With this technology, we can carry on living a normal life identical to how we live now. Each day will be new. We'll age, grow old, and die. The circle of life will go on."

"This all sounds too good to be true," Harper says. "I'm afraid of an unforeseen flaw somewhere. Some sort of defect that will cause this virtual world to come tumbling down, and all of us will cease to exist."

"There are built-in safeguards that will protect us that I will explain in detail when we return to the off-site lab," Robert replies. "This concludes our tour, so now we will return to the transfer hub."

We transfer back to the off-site lab and awaken in our physical bodies. I reluctantly revert back to being captive in my wheelchair.

We go to a small meeting room to discuss our experience of gaining an in-depth understanding of the project and see if the general consensus is to agree or disagree with the feasibility of living in a virtual world. Robert will address any concerns that the Leadership Council members may have in an attempt to put their minds at ease.

"I hope you enjoyed your tour and now realize that we can, in fact, live in a virtual world that emulates our real world perfectly," Robert says. "During your visit to the VE site, you were, in effect, living virtually."

"I'm very impressed with this facility," Vivian replies. "I've never felt better than I did when we were at the VE site. Normally, I feel pain in my left ankle while walking, but it seemed to be absent. Robert, is that to be expected?"

"Yes. It's because the network has no record of your chronic ankle pain. How are the rest of you feeling now that you've experienced an out-of-body state for a few hours?" Robert asks, his eyes moving from one person to the next.

"Well, I'll admit that I didn't feel any different than I do now," Harper says. "How can we be reassured that a VE system failure can't occur?"

"Many of the supporting systems have safeguards built in," Robert explains. "There's redundancy built into the power grid, for instance. Right now, we have six solar feeds from the solar array up in space. We can survive on any one of the feeds, if necessary. We also have twenty-one memory pillars, but we use only fourteen of them. The remaining pillars act as a back-up if any of the pillars should fail. Another example of redundancy is the control centre. It has twelve server towers available, but we only require four to operate. Also, everything is monitored carefully to ensure our safety."

"I am willing to agree that VE is reasonably well protected," Harper says, "but I still have some issues with the thought of living virtually. Would we at some point return to physically living in the real world?"

"Yes, that is definitely our hope," Robert replies.

"How long are we expected to live in VE if such an eventuality arises?" Marek asks.

"We have designed VE to operate for up to one thousand years depending upon the duration of environmental recovery," Robert replies.

"We have to talk more about this project after we return to New Washington," Harper says. "I'm not prepared to endorse VE just yet."

"I agree with you, Harper," Robert says. "It will take some time to weigh all of the pros and cons of living in VE. Unless there are any further questions, this meeting is adjourned."

They return to their rooms to relax and contemplate their reaction to what they have seen. The return trip to New Washington is uneventful, and Robert schedules a meeting for the following day at 9:00 a.m.

CHAPTER 17

All of the Leadership Council members are present as Robert enters the conference room. After Robert greets them, Harper feels compelled to jump in and state her views on the VE project.

"The fact that all of the population will physically die in order to transition over to VE is unacceptable. We're, in effect, intentionally murdering thousands of people to, quote, 'live in a better world.' In this case the term 'live' is subject to a new definition of what it means to be alive."

"What you say makes sense," Forrest replies. "But what if we were all going to die anyway? Shouldn't we try to survive by any means possible?"

"I know that migrating over to VE is a very controversial topic," Robert says. "It is possible, however, to have VE fully operational with the populations of both cities going about their business in the same manner as they would in the real world. My point is that if there is a situation where we must react quickly to a life-support crisis, VE would continue as our safe refuge. We have toured the off-site base and VE, and further to that, may I suggest that we take a behind-the-scenes tour of the VE software platform in beta test mode and witness how life can go on the same way as we're living today."

"Yes, let's do that," Vivian says. "I need to see that living in VE is exactly like living in the real world."

"So, VE becomes a temporary extension of reality until such time that we can return to reality?" Forrest asks.

"Yes, well said, Forrest," Robert replies. "Living in VE is only temporary. We now have the capability to mirror in some or all of the population of New Washington to demonstrate that the way we live today will not change. The population that is mirrored in are fully conscious inside VE and not just replicated. They are mentally making decisions and reacting to the same stimuli as the people in the real world."

"I am still struggling with this concept, so you need to convince me that our sense of humanity will not be lost, and we won't become a population of virtual robots," Harper says.

"I completely understand where you're coming from," Robert replies. "However, our behind-the-scenes tour of VE will allow you to witness life in our newly created world. What you are about to see is the general population mirrored into VE in parallel with their existence in the real world. A unique feature of the VE operating platform is that it allows us to occupy Virtual Earth in stealth mode, so we can neither be seen nor heard as we observe the population doing what they normally do."

"That's amazing," Forrest says. "We can see and hear them, but they don't know that we're there?"

Robert smiles. "That's correct. We can converse with and see each other, but we are in a separate dimension or strata from the general population."

The Leadership Council members follow Robert and me to the transfer hub, which is located on the Research Institute's lower level.

"Please enter a cubicle and follow the instructions on the monitor," Robert says. "See you in VE."

We each enter a separate cubicle located around the perimeter of the transfer hub and make ourselves comfortable in the reclining chairs with raised clear canopies. Robert assists me into my chair. Once seated, the canopies close and a small dose of happy gas is administered, putting us to sleep. Once we're individually transformed into stealth mode, we meet Robert to begin our tour. We feel as if we're in a cloud surrounded by a white haze. Robert instructs us to close our eyes and to keep them closed until told to open them.

After a few seconds, Robert directs the group to open their eyes, and we take a first look at our new world. We're suspended above the New Washington promenade, a scene that is quite familiar to the group. Down below, people are enjoying their day, as usual. The sidewalk cafés are busy, and everyone seems to be in a cheerful mood.

"As you can see, everything is the same as it is in the real world," Robert explains.

We're pleasantly engrossed in observing life in the virtual environment. Members of our group remark that they can't believe we're not actually in the real world.

We briefly pay a visit to a virtual representation of New Los Angeles, and everything is the same there. Life seems to carry on as per usual, just like in the real world.

"Robert, I want to see my family before we end the tour," Harper says. "I need to know how they're doing."

"No problem," Robert replies. "Close your eyes and then open them when I tell you to."

After a few seconds, Robert instructs Harper to open her eyes, and her family members are viewable in different locations, their images appearing in separate bubbles.

"I can see them!" Harper says. "My husband is at work, and my kids are doing their schoolwork at home with the older one, as usual, sitting at his desk somewhat distracted. He's looking at his favourite action hero e-poster. My daughter is working diligently at her desk as well. Robert, I'm so happy to know that life in VE mimics the real world so perfectly."

Other members of the group see their families as well. Then we return to the transfer hub and exit stealth mode.

"Judging by your demeanour," Robert says, "you are suitably impressed with and perhaps even pleasantly surprised that living in a virtual world is pretty great."

"The fact that your virtual world looks so real does not negate the fact that if we migrate there, all of those people, including my family, will be physically dead," Harper says.

"Harper is right," Vivian pipes up. "We need to discuss this with the populations of both cities and gain their buy-in."

The next morning, Robert and the leadership councils gather in the conference room next to the president's office to finish their discussion. The lively pre-meeting discussions are interrupted as the meeting is brought to order.

"Welcome, everyone," Thomas says. "We're gathered here today to, hopefully, reach a consensus on proceeding with preparations to migrate to VE if needed."

"Now that you've witnessed a simulated VE operating state, I hope that you have gained a greater confidence level regarding what it's like to live in a virtual environment," Robert adds. "Keep in mind that we're left with few options to save the population from certain death if our life-support systems fail."

"Your virtual world is truly a marvel of engineering," Harper says, "but I still maintain we have no right to kill the population. I, for one, can't endorse such a strategy. What do the rest of you think?"

"I think I would rather live in a virtual environment than simply die and end my existence along with the rest of the population," Forrest says.

"But my question is, are we really alive in VE?" Vivian asks.

"An excellent question," Robert replies. "There are plans to re-emerge into the real world after the environment has had time to recover. Another point I would like to make is that the life-support systems currently in use will not outlast the reparation period required for the environment to recover. We don't have a guaranteed back-up plan, and our long-term survival is not assured."

"Robert is right," Marek says. "It may take hundreds of years for the environment to recover."

"OK, enough talk," Harper cuts in. "I think we should have a secret ballot to say yay or nay to the concept of living in VE. I also think we should make the general population aware of the prospect of living in a virtual world."

"Please be careful to assess all of the facts before making your decision," Thomas cautions. "What we decide today will have a far-reaching impact regarding where we focus our research resources in the future."

The outcome of the vote is a split decision with two members saying yes and two saying no to using VE as a fail-safe if the life-support systems fail.

"I'm sorry to hear that you don't agree with using VE as a back-up," Robert says. "We'll stop all activities related to VE until we determine if the general population endorses living in a virtual world."

CHAPTER 18

Following the meeting, the Research Institute personnel are notified that the VE project has been temporarily halted, and all data files are to be archived. I'm devastated knowing that tissue-regrowth research will stop as well and angry because I must remain in isolation. During my time alone, Stanley tells me that he has been in contact with the Freedom Alliance rebels and that they want to sabotage the NW and NLA life-support systems. I remember one of the men who mentioned VE passing by me in the hallway, and I decide that I need to speak with him.

The next day I'm in the lab tidying up my bench when I spot the man who mentioned VE while passing by, and he is chatting with another lab technician. As he turns to walk away, I wave at him and summon him over to my bench.

"Hi. I'm Allan, and you're Kaylee," he says. "I remember speaking with you briefly a while ago."

"Hi. Yes. I remember. I have a question for you," I reply.

"Shoot," Allan says.

"Do you know a guy named Stanley? He's a—"

I stop as Allan motions me to be silent. "You know Stanley?" he whispers.

"Yes, I know him. We're good friends. I'm the one who tried to contact Jess Spencer."

It's the end of the workday, and everyone has left for the day, so Allan and I are alone.

"Maybe you can help me. I want to help the Freedom Alliance rebels with their plans to attack the NW and NLA life-support systems and force the VE project to resume," I say.

Allan nods. "OK. I can send you the link that will allow you to contact them."

"Thank you."

As Allan departs, I just hope that I'm doing the right thing.

CHAPTER 19

Meanwhile at the rebel base, it has been decided that now is the time to attack the New Washington and New Los Angeles oxygen-enhancement facilities. Juan and his commanding officers choose six personnel who will form two groups of three to carry out the mission. Two of the men have had special ops experience and look forward to their assignments.

"We're going to attack the New Washington and New Los Angeles oxygen-enhancement facilities," Juan announces. "Jess, I know you're new, but you need to gain some operations experience. Just be aware that this is a high-risk mission."

"But I—"

"Don't contradict me, Jess," Juan warns. "You need to do this!"

The New Washington team consists of Jess, who is twenty-seven years old and lacks any military experience; Owen Kish, who is thirty-six years old with ten years of military service; and Divesh Bhatt, a forty-three-year-old who is very enthusiastic but lacks any military experience.

The New Los Angeles team consists of Tyrell Lewis, an African American with twelve years of military service; Curtiss Smith, a thirty-nine-year-old with no prior military experience; and Seth Brown, who is forty-five years old and also has no previous military service.

They are briefed that evening regarding the details of the timing, strategy, and equipment needed to execute their mission.

Tyrell, Curtis, and Seth hop a freight train as it travels from New Washington to New Los Angeles. Their departure is timed so that they can steal an armoured six-wheeled, all-purpose troop transport vehicle, one of several that are being transported on flatcars to New Los Angeles to be refurbished. They easily gain entry into one of the APT vehicles and wait for the train to slow down as it passes through a rail yard just outside of New Los Angeles. Having previously removed the vehicle's tie downs, they wait until they are stopped next to an unloading dock. Then they drive off the flatcar to make their escape.

That evening at dusk, Jess, Owen, and Divesh travel by truck and, after two days of travelling non-stop, arrive at a location in the desert just outside of the secure zone that protects New Washington's oxygen-enhancement facility. Both groups are now in position and ready to proceed with their nocturnal mission.

At 2:30 a.m., the New Washington team deploys a camouflage tarp that forms a canopy over their vehicle. Its purpose is to fool the security drones that patrol the secure area continuously. As they draw nearer to the target, the New Washington team's monitoring equipment detects a remote security installation located in the desert up ahead that includes a camera and a vibration sensor. Owen delegates Jess to deal with the security installation.

Feeling uneasy, Jess crawls on her stomach and places a compact video monitor with a downward-looking camera in front of the security camera lens. The security camera now has a view of the sand directly below the monitor. Trying to remain calm, she pours a green gel-like substance over the vibration sensor to neutralize it and then quickly returns to the vehicle. Owen offers Jess a hearty congratulations on a job well done.

They stop momentarily while a security drone flies overhead. Then they encounter two more remote security monitors. Owen and Divesh neutralize them. When they see the glow of white light over the next ridge, they realize they have reached their target. Feeling confident, they depart their vehicle and approach the top of the ridge to survey the level of activity at the facility.

The facility is set apart from the domed supporting building and is connected via a covered roadway that looks to be about 200 feet long. No workmen or security personnel are visible. Divesh remains at the top of the ridge to serve as a lookout.

Following a comms check, Owen and Jess approach the perimeter fence. They are hidden from view by a pair of refrigerant storage tanks. They exchange their oxy-pack nasal apparatus for fully enclosed face masks with dual air filters to protect themselves should they come into contact with toxic refrigerant fumes. Then they dig under the perimeter fence and affix time-delayed explosives to one of the cooling towers and each of the refrigerant storage tanks.

After that, they split up and place explosives in the refrigerant manufacturing building as well as the attached compressor refurbishment centre and spare parts warehouse. Divesh keeps a sharp lookout for any personnel movements, ready to inform Jess and Owen of any pending danger. The time delayed explosives on the refrigerant storage tanks have nearly run out of time and will detonate in less than five minutes.

As Jess and Owen crawl up the sand dune behind the refrigerant storage tanks to join Divesh, they are spotted by a drone. When they are about to jump into the truck and leave, they hear an aircraft approaching. It shines a bright searchlight on them, and six armed men dressed in hazmat suits confront them, demanding their surrender. Jess, Owen, and Divesh are ushered on board the hovercopter and depart just before the storage tanks blow, spewing toxic refrigerant high into the atmosphere. The remaining explosives detonate minutes later, causing extensive damage to the oxygen-enhancement facility.

The men at the New Los Angeles facility complete their tasks in a timely manner as well, placing their explosives throughout the facility, then prepare to depart. As they approach the perimeter fence where they gained entry, a drone flies overhead and detects them. Alarm bells sound, and a jeep carrying four security guards wearing hazmat suits approaches the intruders. A spotlight is focused on the pair, and a loudspeaker orders them to drop their weapons and lay face down. They along with Seth, their lookout, are quickly arrested. Sniffer drones and all available personnel are deployed to locate the explosive charges and deposit them in armoured munitions-disposal cases. The cases are quickly loaded onto a remote-controlled flatbed service truck that is sent out into the desert just in time for the explosives to detonate. Tyrell, Curtis, and Seth are taken into custody.

CHAPTER 20

Thomas is immediately contacted by security and told that the oxygen-enhancement facility has been heavily damaged by saboteurs. He alerts the leadership councils of an emergency meeting. They meet virtually within the hour.

"We have an emergency situation," Thomas begins. "New Washington's oxygen-enhancement facility was attacked last night. The refrigerant storage tanks, the compressor refurbishment centre, and Cooling Tower Two were heavily damaged. New Los Angeles was attacked as well, but security was able to thwart the attackers, and their facility is undamaged."

"Are we in imminent danger?" Harper asks. "Should we sound the alarm?"

"No, we're not in immediate danger," Thomas continues. "I don't think that sounding the alarm is a good idea. We could have a mass panic situation. "

"But I assume that the population of New Washington is now at risk with few options to explore," Forrest says.

"Yes, you are correct," Thomas admits. "Robert, in light of what has happened, what's our next step?"

"The only option available to us at this time is for us to prepare to migrate to Virtual Earth on short notice. This can happen if the Leadership Council will reverse its decision and endorse VE. The VE project is complete and can be rapidly deployed."

The room is silent for several seconds.

"Let's have a show of hands if you endorse using VE as our fail-safe in the event of a catastrophic life-support system failure."

"That's like asking us if we should launch the life rafts as the ship is sinking," Forrest says. "We don't have much of a choice, do we? I vote in favour."

The remaining members of the Leadership Council slowly raise their hands as well.

"I want you to know that the only reason I agree with your plan is for my kids," Harper says. "I can't bear the thought of them being poisoned by contaminated air."

"Robert, pull out all the stops and have your team do whatever it takes to be ready to migrate over to VE," Thomas says. "Meeting adjourned."

CHAPTER 21

Unaware of the calamitous events that have taken place that threaten New Washington's very existence, I am planning to carry out one final experiment on myself that should fix my spinal cord. It is 1:33 a.m. as I depart from my apartment. After avoiding being detected by security drones, I arrive at the Research Institute.

Upon entry into the medical research lab, I shut off the overhead lights to avoid detection and then proceed to my cubicle. To disguise my identity, I enter my alias username and password to log into the Research Institute's computer network. Stanley created for my use an alternate username and password so I would have access to the Research Institute computer network if for some reason I am denied access. I copy a mixture of some updated computer files along with some new files from my memory module over to the Research Institute server. The plan is to perform one last procedure on myself that will hopefully allow me to walk. I know I'm taking a huge risk, but I assure myself that I have double-checked my calculations and have nothing to worry about.

After I enter the operating room, I mentally prepare myself for the procedure. I download the updated files from the Infinium computer system to the prototype fixture-control module. Next, I load intelligent nano-probes suspended in a saline fluid into a syringe attached to the robotic arm mounted on the prototype fixture next to the operating table. After partially disrobing to expose my lower spine, I lower the operating table and pull myself onto it, lying face down, then press the button to raise the table. Once I'm in place, I use an alcohol swab to sanitize the area where the syringe will penetrate my lower back. Next, I connect the robotic fixture communication cable to my uplink port and position a transparent face mask that covers my mouth and nose that will supply me with happy gas. The uplink port will use intelligent nano-probes already resident in my brain from earlier experiments.

After pressing the green "start" button on the fixture, I am gassed into a deep sleep, and the syringe penetrates deeply into my lower spine at the targeted location, releasing the nano-probes. The needle retracts, and the process proceeds as before, but this time, it completes the operation. The operating room lights switch on as I slowly awaken, straining my senses to tell if I have any feeling in my legs and feet. I move my left leg with difficulty until my foot contacts the bedrail, and I can feel the coolness of the steel tubing.

"I moved my leg! I can feel it! I can feel my foot touching it!" I exclaim.

With tears welling up, I remove my face mask and uplink port communication cable. Next, the operating table bed is lowered so my feet can touch the floor. I'm still feeling a little groggy, but I'm also elated that I can feel my legs and feet. It is a strange and unfamiliar sensation to me. With my legs dangling over the side of the bed, I swing them for a minute or two, letting my feet brush the cool floor and wondering what it will feel like to walk.

Trying to stand is more challenging than I thought. I immediately fall to the floor. Tears of disappointment flow from my eyes, and I start to sob. But then I realize that I have never used my leg muscles, so they are likely severely atrophied. After I regain my composure, I pull myself over to my wheelchair and struggle to be seated. After getting dressed, I go to the storeroom and bring someone's abandoned crutches to my desk so I can try to do some leg muscle toning exercises. It's so wonderful to be able to feel every bit of leg movement. Then I archive my computer files onto the Research Institute's server and log out of the computer network, feeling overjoyed knowing that my tissue-regrowth process works.

Suddenly, the lab entrance door flies open, surprising me. As I swing around in my wheelchair, some of the lab lights switch on, and I see the silhouettes of three people approaching my cubicle, giving me a sick feeling in the pit of my stomach.

Nikita Novikov, New Washington's chief immigration officer who also is tasked with some security duties, approaches me, followed by one male and one female security guard.

"Recently, we have been monitoring the unauthorized use of the lab equipment, and we were alerted that the operating equipment in this lab was in use this evening," Nikita says. "Did you perform any procedures?"

"Yes," I reply sheepishly.

"Speak up! I can't hear you!"

I lower my head. "Yes, I did."

Nikita looks at me with her piercing eyes as I sink deeper into my wheelchair.

"You do realize that you are not authorized to use the lab equipment to perform experiments on yourself and that there will be consequences."

"But I—"

"Don't interrupt me!" Nikita shouts. "A report will be forwarded to your superiors, and they will determine what course of action will be taken. Until then, you will be escorted to your apartment, where you'll remain until further notice."

Nikita departs immediately, and the security guards accompany me home.

Sobbing while staring at the blank wall of my darkened room with the curtains drawn, I feel utterly depressed. Knowing that I may be banned from the Research Institute will surely dash any hope of continuing to be involved with medical research projects. Just then my communicator beeps with an incoming call. It's Robert. I'm reluctant to answer, but I do anyway.

"Kaylee, Kaylee, Kaylee," Robert says, "What am I going to do with you? I know what you're trying to do, and I can't blame you for trying. I'm sure you're aware of the risks you're taking, but you can't do that in the name of the

Research Institute. We have a strict code of conduct that must be followed, not to mention a reputation to uphold."

I try to stop sobbing and pull myself together enough to respond.

"I know I shouldn't have experimented on myself, but being stuck in a wheelchair tortures me all day, every day. It's like a life sentence with no escape."

"I know you're in a difficult predicament, and I'll see what I can do to minimize the penalty," Robert says, "but I make no promises. You have committed a serious offence. Try to not be too hard on yourself, and get some rest. Let me know if you need anything."

"I will. Thanks for calling, and yes, I'll get some rest."

CHAPTER 22

After secretly exercising my leg muscles for two days, I can't understand why I'm still unable to walk without the assistance of crutches.

Early the next morning, I receive a notification that I'm to be relocated and to pack my belongings in preparation to be escorted to my new domicile. As I finish packing, there is a knock at my door.

"Security!" a female voice announces.

I open my door and see one male and one female security officer. Coincidentally, they're the same two who escorted me to my room from the lab when I was placed under house arrest.

"Are you ready to go?" the male security guard asks.

"Yes. Where are we going?"

"You'll see soon enough," the female guard says.

The male guard pushes me in my wheelchair through the promenade to a warehouse adjacent to the hovercopter apron and deposits me in a small waiting room close to the hangar door. The air is warm and stale with little inflow of fresh air, making me feel drowsy. I fidget with the bracelet Jess made for me, wondering how she's doing. A short while later, a young man with a pleasant smile enters the waiting room.

"If you need to use the facilities, please do it now," he says. He departs as fast as he appeared.

Five minutes later, he reappears wearing an oxy-pack and carrying one for me. "You need to put this on so we can go outside."

"Where am I going?" I ask.

He doesn't reply. Instead, he helps me fit the oxy-pack and then grabs my carry-on bag and pushes me out of the waiting room onto the tarmac. We exit the warehouse through the open hangar door and head toward a freight hovercopter with the loading ramp lowered. Now I am really confused. *Where are they taking me?* I wonder.

Once on board, my wheelchair is secured in place, and a tie-down strap is used to affix me to my wheelchair in the event of turbulence or any other sudden movements. I'm beyond worried, not knowing where I'm going or why. I receive a message on my communicator.

"Miss Kaylee Parker. After due consideration, it has been decided that the punishment for disobeying the New Washington Research Institute lab usage directives is to expel you from New Washington to parts unknown. You are prohibited from making contact with any parties within New Washington from this day forward."

Needless to say, I am devastated. It appears that my destiny is to be left out in the desert to die alone. I begin to sob.

A few minutes later, to my surprise, three more people with bags over their heads are brought on board and seated on metal military jump seats next to me. They are all wearing dishevelled khaki clothing and weathered black high-sided boots. Their escort removes the bag from one of the prisoners, and he is stunned to see someone else in the cargo hold.

"Hi, little lady. You're not who I was expecting to see," Divesh says.

Before I have a chance to reply, the bag is removed from prisoner number two. He's also surprised to see me and my wheelchair.

"Whoa, another outcast?" he says. "Hi, I'm Owen."

I'm mesmerized by his good looks and his charming voice. He stares back at me too, although he tries not to make it too obvious.

"Hi, Owen, I'm Kaylee. I guess I'm an outcast. I thought I was travelling alone. I'm so glad to have some company. Do you know where we're going?"

Owen shakes his head. "No. All I know is we're being booted out of New Washington."

"Why?"

"We were arrested after setting the charges that destroyed the NW oxygen-enhancement facility."

After a brief delay, the bag is removed from the third person. As soon as I see her, I'm shocked and amazed.

"Jess!"

"Kaylee!"

Owen looks back and forth between us. "I take it you two know each other?"

"Yes, yes," I reply. "We've been friends forever!"

The hovercopter pilot pokes his head into the cargo bay and announces that we will be departing in five minutes.

He also gives each of us a flask of water and a snack. Once the cargo bay door closes, we find ourselves in tight quarters with not much space to move about. There is little in the way of lighting, with two small overhead lamps shining down on us. We hear the roar of the rotors revving to maximum and then reducing briefly. Departure is smooth. We feel the aircraft bank to the right and then level off. One hour and forty-five minutes later, the pilot reappears.

"We're landing in about five minutes. Put on your oxy-packs and prepare to deplane," he says.

The hovercopter lands smoothly and the cargo bay door is lowered. The sunlight is blinding, and the heat is intense. Owen removes my seatbelt and wheelchair restraints and pushes me down the ramp onto the soft sand. The wheelchair is difficult to move for a few feet until we reach a hard-packed surface. Jess brings my carry-on bag and watches as the pilot drops off an orange case.

"Have fun!" he says.

We cover our faces as the hovercopter departs, causing a minor dust storm as it lifts off. Soon it disappears from sight.

Our new surroundings consist of a flat, barren landscape with red rock mountains in the distance. There is no sign of life anywhere, and we have no idea where we are.

"I'm not sure, but some of the landscape looks vaguely familiar," Owen says.

"I was hoping they were sending us to an all-inclusive resort," Jess jokes. "All we seem to be missing is the resort!"

"Let's check out the orange case," Divesh suggests. "It looks like an emergency survival kit."

We open the case to find wide-brim khaki sun hats, military rations, oxy-pack cartridges, safety flares, and flasks of water to sustain us until we find a place of refuge. However, I think they just left us to die. Maybe they should have simply executed us instead of making us suffer. With no place in particular to go, we follow the hard-packed surface west toward the ridge of mountains in the distance.

After about two hours, we're taking a break when we see a dust trail looming in the distance and growing larger with each passing second.

"Hey, I think that dust trail is from a truck," Owen says.

"How can we get their attention?" Jess asks.

"What if they're not friendly?" I ask. "What if they want to kill us for our food?"

Divesh stands up. "Well, there's only one way to find out."

He sets off one of the flares, and a blazing flash of bright pink light arches across the sky above us. However, it appears that they did not see the flare, as the dust trail diminishes in the distance. Then, to our surprise, we see something in the distance and soon hear the sound of a truck approaching. It's a military tanker truck. We gather together in a defensive position as the truck nears and toots its horn a few times. Then the truck stops, and Brad, Owen's friend, jumps out of the cab and runs toward us.

"Owen, Jess, Divesh, I thought you guys were dead! Where the hell did you come from, and what are you doing here? Also, who's the girl?"

Brad has a sparkle in his eyes as he glances at me. I admit he's quite handsome.

"Whoa. Too many questions. We blew up the New Washington oxygen-enhancement facility and got caught," Owen explains. "They dumped us out here, probably expecting us to die. And I don't know why Kaylee is with us."

"I performed unauthorized experiments on myself to try to fix my spinal cord and was busted," I explain.

"You guys on a water run?" Jess asks.

"Yeah, just heading back to base," Brad replies. "Let's get going. It's too damn hot out here!"

Minutes later, I'm seated next to Brad, who is in the driver's seat, along with Jess while the others sit or stand wherever they can find a safe place. My wheelchair is folded and secured to the truck's rear bumper. The ride back to base takes us across barren, uneven terrain, causing us to rock from side to side. The ride is long and hot but uneventful, allowing Jess and I to catch up on what has been happening since we last saw each other.

"You left New Washington without telling me?" I ask.

"You had disappeared, and I didn't know how to reach you."

"I tried to contact you using the darknet, but they said you weren't in the New Washington directory."

Jess nods. "I had to leave. They were going to force me to have an uplink port installed. There's no way I'm having one of those things invade my brain."

"Well, at least we're able to see each other, even if the circumstances aren't ideal," I reply.

Jess smiles and squeezes my shoulders. "I'm glad we met up too."

CHAPTER 23

Immediately following the emergency Leadership Council meeting, Robert contacts Alexa Verselado, Virtual Earth's one-site project leader. "Hello, Alexa. We have an emergency situation unfolding in NW that we can't resolve, so we need to prepare Virtual Earth to go live as soon as possible. You can access the 'Go Live' prep procedure at your workstation. I'm giving your team forty-eight hours to finalize the uniformity of the plasma coating and then prepare for system power up."

"Robert," Alexa replies in surprise. "Why are we going live so soon? We have more system testing to complete before we'll be sure that everything is working as it should."

"The New Washington oxygen-enhancement facility was heavily damaged by rebels, and our life-support air supply is on the verge of a catastrophic failure," Robert explains. "We have no spare parts left to draw upon to make further oxygen-enhancement system repairs, which puts us at risk. Alexa, I need you to let me know if there are any issues preventing us from migrating to VE. Please message me with your preparation status as you reach each key checkpoint."

"OK, Robert. We'll work as fast as we can to complete preparations to go live, and I'll keep you posted with the status of each step. Bye for now."

Alexa calls a meeting of the Virtual Earth team and informs them of the urgent need to prepare to go live but withholds the reason why. The plasma coating touch-ups and testing continue overnight and are completed the following day. Next, Alexa directs the construction crew to remove the plasma spray arm assemblies as well as all associated scaffolding and temporary work platforms. The removal takes another day and a half. Various sections of the sphere's open-grid flooring are also removed, exposing the tops of the memory pillars. Alexa gives Robert a final update, stating that they are ready to go live.

Cooling Tower Two's compressor is damaged and overheating and suddenly erupts in a violent explosion, setting off an alarm in the control centre. The technicians scramble to get into their hazmat suits and rush over to the cooling tower so they can shut it down and close all vents to prevent the possibility of toxic refrigerant gas entering the domes. However, the door to the cooling tower is jammed and won't open. They try to force it, but the door refuses to budge. The explosion also ruptured the 200-gallon refrigerant gas reservoir used to top up the system when the compressors are replaced. To make matters worse, the refrigerant gas reservoir is gravity fed from a 2,000-gallon central refrigerant tank, located next to Cooling Tower Two with the shut-off valve located inside the cooling tower's control room. Visibility in the cooling tower is almost nil due to the escaping refrigerant gas, dust, and smoke from the compressor explosion. All of the cameras inside the cooling tower are rendered useless, unable to assess the extent of the damage. The techs can see refrigerant gas seeping from under the door and notify their supervisor, Dan Brinker. He calls Robert immediately.

"Robert, all hell has broken loose here! Cooling Tower Two's compressor blew, and refrigerant gas is escaping from the 200 gallon reservoir. The entry door is jammed shut, and we can't gain access to close the dome's air vents. Also, all control circuitry is out of commission, so there's no way we can remotely close the vents."

"I have Thomas Williams on the line," Robert replies. "The air in the domes will become contaminated within minutes. Thomas, put on your emergency breathing apparatus now. Dan, do what you can to close the cooling tower vents and then report back to me."

At 2:38 a.m., most of the population of New Washington is fast asleep when they are unexpectedly awakened by alarms. As people try to come to grips with the situation, wondering why the alarm has sounded, the air is already being poisoned with highly toxic refrigerant gas.

Masses of people exit their buildings and enter the central dome, trying to escape the toxic fumes. Hordes of people move throughout the promenade in search of an escape, but none can be found. They struggle to breathe as they cry for help, but no help is in sight. Everyone is coughing and gasping, pushing one another aside as they try to find a better place. Some people fall to the ground, too weak to move, and are trampled by others. To make matters worse, their vision is impaired as well by the poisoned air. The darkened atmosphere in the domes is a sultry green colour due to the refrigerant gas, and the smell is rancid.

CHAPTER 24

Thomas and Robert conclude that they have no choice but to transition the population over to Virtual Earth before it's too late.

Thomas walks over to his office window, and all he can see is a green fog blanketing the promenade, partially obscuring his view of the people gathered there.

"Robert, I can see thousands of people out in the promenade looking for an escape from the poisoned air," he says over his communicator. "Many have fallen to the ground, and I can't tell if they're dead or alive."

"We have to move quickly to keep the suffering to a minimum," Robert replies. "Thomas, once you have your breathing apparatus on and functioning, retrieve the briefcase marked with an 'M' from your wall safe."

"OK, I have it," Thomas says a few minutes later.

"Now open it," Robert instructs. "The display will power up automatically and prompt you for a security code. You will receive the thirteen-digit code directly through your uplink port. Enter the code and then let me know when you're done."

Thomas does exactly as he's told. "The display has changed to a different screen. It's prompting me to enter a date and time."

"Good. We have to set a starting point for the Virtual Earth time clock to commence. We need to set the clock at one minute past midnight on the day before the oxygen-enhancement facility was destroyed. That will allow life to continue normally for the general population with no recollection of what has transpired in the last five days. Thomas, only you and I will be aware of our migrating the New Washington population over to VE."

"Are you sure this will work?" Thomas asks. "It's like we're manipulating time, as if we're inside a time machine."

"In a manner of speaking, you're right. We have to reset the clock, and we can do so for up to seven days. All necessary data to do this has been archived in the Infinium computer system. Let's continue."

"The display now shows a large green icon with the word 'start' in the middle of the icon," Thomas says.

"Yes. Touch the icon once, and you'll be prompted one final time after that, asking if you want to continue."

"I have to tell you, Robert, I've never been more nervous in my entire life than I am now. I'm touching the icon now."

Both men are silent for a few seconds. Then Thomas continues, "I'm confirming my start request now."

"Good. Now watch your Virtual Earth status screen to follow the VE start-up sequence, and we will both follow it as it progresses. First, we have to power up Virtual Earth."

Nothing happens for a few seconds as the Virtual Earth control system configures for power up. The cooling fans located in the floor and ceiling of the Virtual Earth sphere ramp up to operating speed, and their displays show the status of all the fans and vents.

"Robert, we have a stuck vent affecting the airflow exit path in vent aperture number three," Alexa reports. "The system has automatically activated the de-icing bladders that inflate to attempt to break away the ice blockage. Bladder inflation is now complete, but the blockage is still in place."

There is silence for what seems like an eternity. Robert is very concerned, as they have no time to repair anything.

"The system is activating the vibration sequence and retrying the de-icing bladder sequence," Alexa says. This time the operation is successful. After a short delay, the ventilation system status changes from red to green with full airflow in place. Alexa, Robert, and Thomas all sigh in relief.

"Don't worry," Robert says. "The vents can't be blocked in the future, as warm air exits from them continuously. Next, the power-supply grid is going to power up."

They watch their displays as the power system status shows a "Power-up Sequence Initiated" message. Next, the satellite power-feed indicator shows a green status followed shortly by the Virtual Earth power grid showing a green status as well.

"Now, we're going to observe on the upper-left corner of our displays the powering up of the sphere plasma coating and memory pillars. Sphere power up will be completed first."

A band of dark-blue light appears at the bottom level of the sphere's plasma coating. Soon, it extends upward until the entire surface of the plasma coating is illuminated. The plasma coating goes through various colour changes until it reaches a bright white status. An exterior view of the sphere, which is shown as a small inset image on the upper-right corner of their video displays, shows a bright luminescence lighting up the barren landscape surrounding the sphere on a dark, cold Arctic night.

"Everything is looking good so far," Robert says. "We're about to create the city of New Washington from Infinium computer data files that will reside within the plasma coating on the sphere. Simultaneously, we will copy the entire population's DNA, physical attributes, personality traits, and memory files from the Infinium computer system into the Virtual Earth memory pillars. When we begin the data upload, you'll see the status of the Infinium computer and the VE memory pillars displayed while tracking data movement."

While that is happening, all of the VE physical parameters are continuously monitored, such as sphere integrity, power consumption, power supply performance, sphere cooling, system performance, and site security.

Thomas and Robert see their video displays reconfigure to display the data movement status indicators using bar graphs with other system parameters shown on a narrow vertical sidebar on the left side of their displays.

Data movement begins, and the video displays are busy with changing data rates as data flow ramps up to maximum. Robert, sitting at his desk at the Research Institute, hears the hum from the Infinium computer system growing louder.

The Virtual Earth memory pillars have moved upward from their below-floor position until they almost make contact with the sphere's plasma coating. A series of colour changes are evident, starting at the bottom of each pillar and progressing to the top as each pillar is populated with data files. The pillars start off with an indigo blue and transition to yellow with orange waves, to red with white waves and then the red gradually disappears, leaving pure white light. The observers' displays present a colourful light show taking place inside the sphere.

The data files take a few hours to copy over to Virtual Earth, allowing Robert and Thomas time to assess the status of the general population. Thomas once again looks out of his office window and is horrified to see masses of people lying on the ground in the promenade with no movement evident.

"Will we be able to migrate over to VE even if most of the population has died?" Thomas asks.

Robert replies, "Yes, we can migrate over because we are using data archived in the Infinium computer system to virtually create NW and then re-populate by resetting the clock to start before the NW oxygen enhancement system was destroyed."

Suddenly, a flashing red warning message appears on their displays along with a beeping tone as they observe that over ninety percent of the data transfer has been completed.

"Thomas, don't be alarmed," Robert says, "and please pardon the pun. The alarm is a result of the Virtual Earth data buffering levels running a little high, but it will not cause any serious problems. We knew this would happen due to differing computer system file-handling speeds. The file-transfer process should be completed in about an hour."

"Thanks, Robert," Thomas replies. "I was about to have a panic attack! Thankfully, all is well."

"At this point, we have completed all preparatory activities to go live and can soon proceed to move the population from New Washington into Virtual Earth," Robert says. "With all Virtual Earth status indicators showing green, we're ready for the migration to go live."

"Then let's go live now," Thomas says.

"Roger that," Robert replies.

When all of the memory pillars have moved up to engage the sphere's plasma coating, two events take place. First, the city of New Washington goes live within the sphere coating. Second, the human mirroring process begins. All of the population would normally go about their activities as usual in the real world, and their physical appearance plus conscious states would be cloned in Virtual Earth. This means that, under normal circumstances, there would be two parallel living environments active at the same time with one being real and the other an exact duplicate within Virtual Earth. Mirroring would continue for twenty-four hours and, if successful, the migration would be considered complete.

"Given our present situation, we don't have the luxury of using the mirroring feature," Robert says. "The path we're taking now is irreversible. Remember, however, that life within Virtual Earth will be exactly the same as it was in the real world right down to the finest detail."

"What will become of the physical bodies that remain in the real world?" Thomas asks.

"Following the migration, the domes will be filled with a neutralizing gas, causing their bodies to dry out to avoid any unpleasant decomposition issues. The bodies will also have a green tint as a side effect of breathing the refrigerant fumes."

Next, the New Washington infrastructure goes through a computer-controlled shut down. The only exception is the food-production facility, which will continue to function automatically to provide food for the on-site personnel while all other systems are shut down. In addition, some security staff will remain on site following the migration to ensure that all human activity has ceased and that all shutdown tasks have been completed.

His alarm clock announces a new day, and Thomas notices that the date on his communicator now reads five days earlier than it did the night before. He prepares himself for the joint New Washington and New Los Angeles Leadership Council meeting that will take place in a meeting room next to the presidential office. He quickly finishes his breakfast and then embarks on his morning walk around the promenade. There, he hesitates momentarily, reflecting on recent events while taking in the freshness of the morning air amidst the sound of birds chirping in the trees nearby as he views the brightly coloured flowers in the elevated flowerbeds throughout the promenade.

CHAPTER 25

Owen and Brad assist me back into my wheelchair, and we enter the underground rebel base through an airlock, transitioning into a breathable environment and out of the heat. We remove our oxy-packs and proceed down a hallway to an open area with tables and chairs and with a food preparation area off to one side. Juan is seated alone at a table sipping on a drink as we approach.

"Owen, Jess, Divesh, I thought you three were dead!" he says, standing up. "Who's the girl?"

"This is Kaylee Parker," Owen replies. "One of the research scientists from the Research Institute."

Juan tries to suppress a nagging cough and then takes another sip of his drink while staring at me, making me feel uncomfortable. His eyes have the look of a man who has been rejected by the civilized world and is bent on unleashing his anger to destroy the offenders.

"Why were you expelled from New Washington?" Juan asks.

"I was caught performing illegal experiments to try to fix my spinal cord so I can walk."

"It appears that your experiments failed," Juan remarks, his eyes taking in my wheelchair.

"Not completely," I reply. "But right now, all I feel in my legs and feet is pain, and I'm very tired."

Juan has a minor coughing fit resulting from the firestorm damaging his lungs and then sips on his beverage to recover. "Perhaps you should take a painkiller and lie down to rest."

"Yes, that would be great, thanks," I reply.

In the medical treatment room, I am assisted onto a comfortable cot and given a dose of an unknown gas that puts me into a deep sleep.

While resting, I feel the strangest sensation in my legs and feet. It seems like my brain is going through some sort of neural network learning curve.

When I wake up, Owen pokes his head in and he sees me sitting up with my legs dangling over the side of the cot.

"Welcome back! I thought you'd never wake up," Owen says.

"Why? How long was I asleep?"

"Twelve hours. How are you feeling?"

"Great. The pain in my legs is gone, and now I feel that my legs and feet are an active, living part of my body. I think my brain just went through a neural reset to learn to recognize and manage my lower extremities."

"Do you think you can stand?" Owen asks.

I hold my arm out to him. "Let's see."

My first attempt is a failure, and I sit back down on the cot. On my second attempt, however, though I'm a bit wobbly, with Owen's support, I remain standing. I give him a thankful smile, and he smiles back. Then he releases me to stand on my own.

"I did it!" I exclaim. "I'm finally standing on my own two feet, and I can feel all of the movement!"

"Good for you!" Owen says. "With a little exercise to tone your muscles, you should be walking in no time."

After shifting back to my wheelchair, for the first time, I lift my legs and place my feet on the footrests. Owen pushes me down the hallway past the communications office where Juan is talking to someone.

"Who is Juan talking to?" I ask.

"Probably Stanley. They're working on a plan to destroy VE."

"Destroy VE? Why?"

"Juan wants to make sure there's no way they can return to the real world and take control."

"That isn't right. There's no real threat, and I think he's just out for vengeance, plain and simple."

"I wouldn't tell Juan that," Owen warns. "If you do, he'll threaten to shoot you."

"But we have to stop him from destroying VE!" I exclaim.

Later that day, using the communication equipment, I'm able to contact Stanley at the off-site lab. He's glad to hear from me.

"Stanley, I've missed chatting with you. How are you doing?"

"Hi, Kaylee. I've been really busy writing a special, secret program."

"Oh? What sort of program?"

"One that will systematically destroy VE while simultaneously allowing me to use their cameras to watch it happen. I can't wait to deploy it."

"Wow. You're really going to get your revenge on the government, aren't you?"

"Yes. In a few days, when the off-site lab is shut down and all the staff is transferred over to VE, I'll remain here at the off-site lab and hack into the New Washington computer system and run my software."

Just then Juan enters the communications room.

"The communications equipment is off limits!" he shouts. "You should have asked permission to use it. Who were you talking to?"

"My friend Stanley. I know him from when I was working at the off-site base," I reply.

"What did you talk about?" Juan asks, his eyes narrowing with suspicion.

"We reminisced about working together there and how we've missed each other. That's all."

"OK. Now leave this place, and never use this equipment again."

Later that evening, Owen and I are alone in my room. He realizes I'm brooding over something.

"What's bothering you?" he asks.

"I was talking to Stanley earlier today, and he confirmed that he's going to vent his anger with the government by destroying VE."

"How does he plan to do it?" Owen asks.

"He's writing a computer program that will systematically shut down VE, and he says it will take place in a few days."

"Why should we care what happens to VE?" Owen asks. "They wouldn't let us into New Washington in the first place, and two days ago, they abandoned us in the desert."

"I know, I know. It's just that so many innocent people will die."

"They're already dead, in case you didn't know. They're nothing but ones and zeros in some computer system now."

"But they still have a right to exist, don't they?" I ask.

"I suppose they do in some sort of distorted sense of what it means to be alive. So, what can we do to stop him?"

"We need to get to New Washington immediately and shut down the computer system before he runs his software. VE can operate independently without the Infinium computer system to support it. We can sneak out during the night and 'borrow' a truck to travel to NW."

"Yup, we could," Owen says, "but who says I want to save VE? I don't owe them anything."

"OK, then I'll do it myself," I reply. "You can help me into the truck and load my wheelchair in the back so I can drive myself."

"Hold on. I didn't say I wouldn't help you. I was just trying to justify risking my life to save VE."

"So, you'll help me?" I ask, my voice rising with hope.

Owen nods. "Yes. I'll take you to New Washington. Besides, you don't know how to drive. When do we leave?"

"Later tonight when everyone's asleep," I say.

It's 2:30 am, and all is quiet as Owen pushes me in my wheelchair toward the airlock. We put on our oxy-packs and grab oxy-pack refill canisters and some flasks of water before heading out to find a suitable truck. Luckily for us, we see the on-duty security guard leave his post with his girlfriend and disappear to parts unknown. Most of the trucks are unfit for travel or low on fuel, but one of them is ready to go. Owen loads four more jerry cans filled with fuel into the back of the truck, and we quickly depart, hoping no one notices us missing until the morning.

As Owen and I venture farther from the base along the bumpy dirt road, dodging the occasional sand drift, the night air is warm and placid. I use a folded blanket as a pillow and fall asleep for a couple of hours. By daybreak, we finally reach the interstate highway that connects New Los Angeles and New Washington and head south. New Washington is three days away if the road is passable.

When I awaken, the sun is rising to usher in another hot day. I take a few sips of water and notice that my oxy-pack needs a refill, so I make the switch.

"Where were you living before the firestorm?" I ask.

"I was stationed at a military base outside of Los Angeles, participating in combat training exercises," Owen replies.

"How did you end up joining the Freedom Alliance rebels?"

"Brad and I were tasked with rescuing firestorm survivors, and we did find a few. The trouble was, there was nowhere safe to take them, so one of the survivors said he knew of an underground base that would be suitable. When we arrived, Juan and a few others were already there, and they invited us to stay."

"I'm glad you and the others were able to find a safe place," I reply, "but Juan seems to have an extreme hatred for the government and is willing to go to any length to get his revenge."

"True," Owen replies, nodding. "He's a fanatic and will never negotiate with the powers that be. How about you?"

"I enjoyed living in New Washington and working in the Research Institute's advanced medical research department. We were studying tissue-regrowth principles and exploring non-invasive ways to repair damaged or defective human tissue to restore functionality. I broke a few rules by performing unauthorized tissue-regrowth experiments on my spinal cord, and as you know, my punishment was to be expelled from New Washington."

"Jess is going to be really pissed since you left the base without telling her."

"I know, but I couldn't risk telling her in case she ratted on me."

The next morning, one of the rebels approaches Juan as he sits in the cafeteria eating breakfast.

"Juan, one of the trucks is gone! Owen and the girl in the wheelchair are missing too. Do you want us to go after them?"

"What?" Juan shouts.

He breaks into a coughing fit and then drinks his hot morning tea to stop it.

"That girl must have talked Owen into helping her escape," Juan says. "The girl must have found out that

Stanley is planning to destroy VE. Find Brad and Jess, and tell them to come and see me."

"Yes, sir," the man replies.

Brad and Jess appear a few minutes later and await instructions.

"The girl and Owen have escaped, and I suspect they're heading to New Washington to stop Stanley from destroying VE," Juan explains. "Take the jeep, and bring them back dead or alive. They must be stopped. Go now!"

"Kaylee, how could you do this?" Jess asks. "I thought you were on our side."

Brad gets a handgun, and they depart immediately.

While underway they see tire tread marks in the shallow sand drifts that have formed across the road as they continue toward the interstate highway. Heading south, they strain to see if Owen and Kaylee's truck is up ahead. Their jeep is much faster and will allow them to catch up quickly. "Juan might send his men to hunt us down," Owen says. "We'll have to keep checking to make sure no one is after us."

"I'll keep checking," I reply.

The landscape is flat with little vegetation, and the heat is unrelenting. The road's surface is blistered, causing a lot of road noise, and the truck vibrates continuously. There are no signs of life or evidence of any traffic having recently passed through.

A while later, I turn in my seat and check to see if anyone is behind us when I spot something approaching.

"Owen, something is coming, but I can't tell what it is!"

"Here, use the binoculars," Owen replies, handing them to me.

When I focus the binoculars, I can clearly see that it's a jeep. I'm also able to identify the occupants.

"It's Brad and Jess!" I exclaim. "And I don't think it's a social call."

"Better hold on," Owen says. "It could get rough. I'm going to try to run them off the road."

"Oh, Owen, please don't hurt them," I implore.

By then, the jeep is right behind us and preparing to pull along beside. Brad has his handgun in hand and manoeuvres the jeep next to us.

"Owen, stop the truck, or I'll shoot!" Brad demands. "I mean it!"

"OK, OK," Owen replies. "Don't shoot!"

Owen stops the truck and turns off the engine as the jeep stops at an angle in front of us, blocking our escape.

"Get out of the truck," Brad says. "Both of you."

I struggle to lower myself to the ground and go to the driver's side of the truck. Brad points his gun at us as Jess steps forward and slaps me across the face. "I thought you were my friend!" she yells.

I almost lose my balance because my legs are weak. I struggle to straighten up, tears welling in my eyes as I begin to sob. "But I am your friend."

"Liar!" Jess shouts.

"We know where you're going and why," Brad says. "You're planning to stop Stanley from destroying VE, aren't you?"

"Brad, you know as well as I do that we can't stand by and let Stanley destroy VE," Owen says.

"Juan and Stanley have no right to kill over fifty thousand innocent people who pose no real threat to them," I add. "Do you want to live with that on your conscience forever?"

Just then Jess notices that I'm wearing the hand-woven bracelet she gave me. "We're both still wearing our friendship bracelets, and you still treat me like garbage," Jess says. "Some friend you are!"

"OK. Enough talk," Brad says. "Both of you get in the jeep, and we'll let Juan decide what to do with you."

"I can't believe you two would rather be loyal to a murderer," I reply.

Brad ignores my comment. "Kaylee, you can sit in the back with Jess so I can keep an eye on Owen."

With Owen's assistance, I approach the jeep, but as I raise my foot to step up into the rear seat, my foot slips and I fall forward, hitting my knee on the door sill. Brad instinctively reaches over to try to break my fall, and Owen seizes the moment to knock the gun out of Brad's hand and wrestle him to the ground. They struggle on the ground for a few seconds until Brad is subdued.

"Brad, stop struggling! Kaylee, get the gun, and don't let Jess near it."

I take a few steps and, with difficulty, pick up the gun. It's the first time I've held a gun, and it gives me the oddest feeling of power that I have ever felt. Jess looks at me, not knowing if I will use it or not. While keeping an eye on Jess, I retrieve some rope from the truck, and Owen uses it to tie both Brad and Jess to the jeep's front bumper.

"I could have burned the jeep and left you two stranded in the desert, but I won't," Owen says, "I figure that by the time you untie yourselves, we'll be long gone. I'm sure you can come up with an elaborate story to tell Juan to save face and put his mind at ease."

Jess looks at me with hate in her eyes. "You traitor! I hate you, Kaylee! I never want to see you again!"

"You know in your heart that we're doing the right thing," I reply, "and I don't hate you!"

Owen motions me to hand him the gun. Then he moves to the side of the jeep and points it at Brad.

"Owen! Don't shoot!" I scream.

Owen redirects his aim and discharges the gun into the front tire on the driver's side. "That should keep you two out of trouble for a while," he says.

"Thanks," Brad replies. "Oh, and thanks for not leaving us stranded in the desert. We won't try to follow you."

Owen and I return to the truck. After manoeuvring around the jeep, we take one last look at Brad and Jess as we continue on our way. Jess keeps her head down, refusing to look at me.

"Do you think they'll be OK?" I ask.

Owen nods confidently. "I know Brad well enough. They'll survive. I'm not sure what sort of reception they can expect from Juan when they return empty handed, though."

"Yeah, he won't be a happy man."

Owen glances over at me. "How's your knee?"

"It's OK. I guess my weak legs helped us subdue them."

"Well, we had to make a move sooner or later to overtake them, hopefully without anyone being seriously injured or worse."

"I feel bad for Jess," I say, looking in the side mirror. "I hope she didn't mean what she said. I truly don't hate her, and I never could."

Travel for the next little while is uneventful. I keep checking in the mirror to make sure Brad and Jess aren't following us.

Later that afternoon we notice a few tire treads in a shallow sand drift that blankets both lanes of the highway. They have to be recent, or the wind would have erased them, so our curiosity is definitely aroused. It seems like the day will never end as the heat torments us, but the sun finally begins to slide toward the horizon.

"Look! Up ahead!" Owen says. "I see something, but I'm not sure what it is. Do you see it?"

"Yes. And it looks like it's on the road. I wonder what it could be."

As we get closer, we realize it's a military truck with other vehicles stopped ahead of it. Two men are standing at the back of the military truck, their rifles pointing at us.

"Owen. Stop!" I scream.

Owen jams on the brakes, and the truck skids to a stop, both of us unsure if the soldiers mean us harm or not.

"Let's get out slowly and put our hands up to show that we mean them no harm," Owen says.

"That's easy for you to say. My knee hurts, and I don't think I can get out without help."

The two men walk cautiously toward us and then stop.

"Who are you, and what do you want?" one of them asks.

Owen swallows hard, unsure if the men plan to shoot him or not. "We're on our way to New Washington, and we need to get there as soon as possible."

"We've never heard of New Washington. What are you talking about?" the man asks.

"New Washington is a dome-covered city of fifty thousand people about two days southeast of here."

After a few seconds, the tension eases and the men lower their rifles as they approach and greet us. The man who addressed us introduces himself as Wesley. He's tall and slender with a thin face and is wearing khaki military fatigues and sunglasses.

"Hi. I'm Owen, and the young lady in the cab is Kaylee. We're from a paramilitary camp up north, and if we don't get to New Washington in time, many people will die. Who are you people, and where are you going?"

"I'm Zac," one of the other men says. "We're searching for a safe place to settle with a sustainable supply of food, water, and oxygen. Our oxy-pack refill equipment quit working, and if we can't find a suitable place soon, we're going to run out of refills."

Zac has a slim build and is somewhat short. He explains that he is also ex-military and is a communications network technician.

"We have a few extra refills we can give you now, and we also have a portable oxy-pack refilling unit as well," Owen offers.

I wave to the men to come over to my side of the truck.

"I know of a place not far from New Washington that may be suitable for your group," I explain. "It's called

Flatlands National Park. It has an enclosed visitors' centre and staff living quarters attached. When I visited years ago, I remember them telling me that the air smells unusually fresh due to a natural oxygen supply from an unknown underground source."

"Thanks," Wesley says. "I'll discuss that with our group and see what they think of your suggestion. Why don't you two come with us, and I'll introduce you to the other members of our group?"

"Kaylee has some mobility issues, so it would probably be better if I drive up and park where we can gather."

Wesley nods. "OK. Sounds good."

Owen drives past the first two of five vehicles and then rolls to a stop. I open my door and lower myself out of the cab to stand next to the truck so everyone can see me. The convoy consists of a military truck, a tanker truck, an old white Caddy convertible with another tanker behind it, and another military truck bringing up the rear. The group assembles in front of the second tanker, wondering who the strangers are.

"I'd like to introduce you to our visitors," Wesley says. "This is Owen and Kaylee."

Wesley turns and faces us, awaiting an introductory response.

"Hi," I begin, offering a small wave. "Just so you know, we're on a mission. We must travel to a city named New Washington as soon as possible to prevent tens of thousands of people from being murdered."

The group looks at us in confusion, having no idea what I'm talking about.

"While staying at a paramilitary rebel camp, we learned of a plan to shut down a virtual world that houses the entire population of New Washington, a multi-domed city with a population of about fifty thousand people. They were forced to use this virtual world to escape from being killed when their air supply was sabotaged by rebels from our camp. Owen and I plan to stop the rebels from destroying this virtual world by disabling the New Washington Infinium computer system."

There is much discussion amongst the group as they try to comprehend the urgency of our reaching New Washington. Finally, Wesley turns back to us.

"If you're willing to travel with us, we'll help you in any way we can to reach New Washington. Now, I'd like you to meet the members of our group. They are, from left to right, Tyler, Piper, Ronnie, Rosie, Tony, Bernie, Irene, Zac, and Harley. We were living at a little trailer park named Little Eden, but now we have to find a new place to call home."

"As I told Wesley," I say, addressing the group, "I know of a place that might be suitable for your new home. It's located a couple of hours south of New Washington. We can take you there after we finish our mission in New Washington if you'd like."

The group invites us to join them, saying it would be safer to travel with them. We accept their offer, and Wesley announces that we will be leaving in about an hour, once the sun goes down. They only travel at night. Owen offers to take me over to visit with some of the survivors, but I decline. Putting my full weight on my legs, I manage to walk on the soft sand all the way to Bernie, who is holding her Shiatsu, Precious, in her lap. Beside her is Tony, her husband, Owen, and Wesley. I remain standing next to Bernie and do slow knee bends briefly to exercise my leg muscles.

"I see you're having trouble walking," Bernie says.

"I am, but I'm improving steadily. I secretly fixed my spinal cord using the New Washington Research Institute lab and was expelled for performing the procedure without consent."

"Owen, I was thinking," Wesley says. "Maybe it would be a good idea if you and Kaylee travel at the front of the convoy and we bring up the rear since you two know where we're going. We normally go about ten miles per hour if the road is good and no lights."

Owen nods. "Sure. We can do that."

"Is there some way to keep in contact with everyone?" I inquire.

"Yes," Wesley replies. "I'll give you a communicator before we leave. Oh, a rifle and a shotgun too."

"Do we really need the guns?" I ask.

"You never know what we might encounter," Wesley replies. "We have to be prepared to defend ourselves."

"So, Owen, were you in the military at one time?" Tony asks.

"Yes. I was a member of a special-forces team tasked with undertaking the most dangerous missions. We were known as the suicide squad. How about you two? How did you end up here?"

"Well, our home is in New York City, and we were visiting our son when the firestorm hit," Bernie says. "He's a park ranger at Rocky Mountain National Park, and we haven't heard from him since the firestorm."

Precious becomes restless. After Bernie takes her to do her business, the dog hops onto my lap, kissing me on the chin.

"Oh, Precious, you're such a good puppy," I say.

"Now, Precious, you be a good girl and lay down," Bernie orders.

Wesley departs to make his rounds, ensuring that each vehicle is gassed up and ready to go, and Owen moves our truck to the front of the convoy.

CHAPTER 26

As the sun slips behind the western mountain range, the rest of the vehicles fire up, and we move out with the convoy straddling the centreline at a speed of ten miles per hour, as suggested, for most of the night. Having been super-heated when the firestorm passed, the pavement is covered with blisters and often obscured by shallow sand drifts that partially cover the road at times, forcing the vehicles to navigate around them. At one point, the Caddy gets stuck in a deeper sand drift, but the tanker truck behind it pushes it out, minimizing the loss of time. The warm night air initially has a stale musty smell and seems to be oxygen deficient, but it freshens as the night progresses. Without ambient light, the stars put on a spectacular show for everyone to enjoy. The journey is uneventful, though some sheet lightning flashes in the distance to entertain us.

At sunrise, we pull off the highway and into a clearing, forming a circle with our vehicles just like the horse and wagons used to do two centuries before. Harley works his magic and prepares a fine meal, and afterward, the group gathers together to assess our first night of travel.

"So, how did everyone manage last night?" Wesley asks.

Everyone agrees that there were no issues so far, but some are fearful of what lays ahead.

"Travel so far has been good, but we have to be vigilant," Wesley says. "You never know when the unexpected might happen."

"It sure is a lot cooler to travel by night," I remark. "We were sweltering in the midday heat."

"You're lucky your truck didn't overheat," Zac says.

"I can't wait to reach our new home to start a new life," Bernie says.

Everyone thanks Harley for preparing supper. Then they look forward to some well-deserved rest during the oppressively hot daytime hours.

Later in the day, Owen, Zac, and Wesley gas up the vehicles and check them over as we prepare to head out for the next leg of our journey.

We pull out onto the highway just after sunset, continuing south. Shortly after our first rest stop, we head east on a different four-lane divided highway. Fortunately, we encounter few sand drifts, but we do notice a few abandoned vehicles in the ditch and one transport truck on its side, also in the ditch. Once again, however, we have smooth sailing so far.

Lenny, at forty-two years old, is short and pudgy with a round face and poor eyesight in one eye. He is on lookout duty, sitting on top of a sand dune about 300 feet from the main east-west highway and not far from an encampment a few miles away. He takes great pride in his task and claims that he never misses seeing any traffic that passes by. The encampment houses twenty-two residents and is under the control of Boss Man and seven other former prison inmates.

Boss Man's name is Peter Cranberry, but he never goes by that name. As a young lad, he was constantly bullied and had few friends. In high school, three boys in particular, with Shawn being the ringleader, took great delight in mocking him in front of the other students. The taunting continued on a daily basis until Peter had had enough. Peter obtained a weapon that consisted of a set of brass knuckles and a knife. One day after being bullied, Peter retaliated by punching and then slashing Shawn's face. Shawn dropped to the floor, unconscious and bleeding. Peter glared at the crowd of students and was never bullied again.

The inhabitants of the encampment are housed in a former fabrication company structure with a metal truss roof and oxygen-producing equipment on site to refill their oxy-pack canisters. One end of the high-roofed building is open and damaged from the firestorm. Two rail lines enter the building with a wide walkway in between. Inhabitants live in boxcars on both tracks, and a baggage car is situated nearest the loading platform to store supplies and houses the leaders.

A pair of shipping containers are located on the loading platform, spanning between the railroad tracks with the oxygen-producing equipment in behind. The container at the front of the loading platform houses Boss Man, and the one in behind contains the oxy-pack canisters, which remain under lock and key at all times. The inhabitants consist of thirteen men, seven women, and two children. They work either in the greenhouses next door or perform any other supportive tasks to earn their daily oxy-pack canisters.

Lenny is to alert his boss of any passing traffic of interest. He scans the highway periodically with his night-vision binoculars but only rarely spots any traffic. Tonight, will be different.

At 2:20 a.m., he sees something in the distance approaching from the west. He is chewing on one of his homemade pepperoni sticks that he creates using smoked rodent meat and a secret formula of spices he grows himself. At first, it appears to be a single vehicle, but more come into view as they draw closer. Lenny is so excited that he can barely contain himself as he searches through his backpack to retrieve his communicator. He finally finds it and uses it to contact Boss Man's second-in-command, Akello Akee, a former Ugandan mercenary who participated in many atrocities while in Uganda. He emigrated illegally to the US and was convicted of multiple murders, including the killings of men, women, and children.

Lenny takes a deep breath and then spits out the bite-size piece of pepperoni.

"Aky, are you there? Can you hear me? Convoy of vehicles coming. I repeat, a convoy of vehicles coming."

"Yes, mon," Akello replies. "I can hear you, mon. For shit's sake, mon, stop yelling. Now tell me, mon, what exactly do you see?"

"Three military trucks, two tanker trucks, and one car travelling in a convoy. They're moving east with no lights."

"OK, mon. I'll tell the boss and get back to you."

At that very moment, Boss Man is napping in his quarters. Akello knocks on the doorway and then enters.

"Hey, boss. Lenny says there's a convoy of six vehicles headed east."

Boss Man awakens slowly, feeling groggy. "What? Who? A convoy. What do you mean?"

"It's passing by now. There's six vehicles."

Boss Man sits up. "Call the men. Tell them to meet me out by the jeep and to bring their motorbikes."

Once assembled, Boss Man instructs his men to prepare the jeep and designates three men to follow him on motorbikes. They leave immediately, and Akello instructs Lenny to be ready for pickup. By the time they reach the highway, the convoy has just passed. Boss Man gives each of his men specific orders on how they will overtake and capture the convoy.

Ryker, a former prison inmate guilty of killing his wife and her lover, will drive the jeep, and Lenny will be the jeep's munitions man. Corry, a former hit man for the mob, is assigned to capture the Caddy. Hulk, a large muscular man who was imprisoned for killing a man with one punch, is to assist Boss Man with attacking the lead truck. Blade, imprisoned for dismembering a number of people with his machete, is instructed to capture the fuel tanker. They all depart immediately.

After travelling for about an hour after the rest stop, Zac is looking back from the cargo area of the last truck in the convoy when he spots a vehicle approaching fast from the rear. He grabs his communicator. "We got visitors, I repeat, we got visitors. Not sure how many, but they're catching up in a hurry."

"Look alive, everyone," Wesley says. "Have your weapons in hand and be ready to defend yourselves."

As the jeep and four dirt bikes bear down on the convoy, the jeep opens fire with a machine gun.

"Zac! Hang two smoke grenades on the tailgate and pull the pins!" Wesley shouts.

Zac complies and offers return fire but can't see his target clearly due to the smoke. The attackers stop shooting, and the four dirt bikes zoom past Zac and Wesley and head farther up the convoy. The shooter in the jeep resumes shooting briefly and then stops. The smoke cloud starts to diminish, and Zac sees Lenny stand up with a bazooka aimed directly at their truck. Zac tosses two landmines onto the road behind them, but the jeep avoids them. Lenny takes aim with the bazooka and fires. Zac takes cover behind an ammo case.

"Incoming!" he screams. "Take cover!"

Wesley and Zac's truck was damaged during the firestorm and is missing its rear window and windshield, so the shell passes right through the cab and hits the rear doors of Harley's truck. Wesley ducks as flames and shrapnel fly back at him. Harley's truck veers off the road and comes to a stop in the ditch, engulfed in flames. There's nothing Wesley and Zac can do but hope that Harley has survived. As they continue on, Zac sets off two more smoke grenades as the jeep speeds up after slowing to have a look at Harley's truck. Zac tosses out two more landmines, but again the jeep avoids them with little difficulty. Frustrated, Zac hangs another smoke grenade on the tailgate.

As Lenny sets up for another bazooka shot, Zac dumps all six remaining landmines on the road, creating a much more challenging line of defence. The jeep misses the first two mines, but the right-front tire hits the third one spot on. Just as Lenny is about to unleash another bazooka shell, the landmine explodes, tossing the right side of the jeep high into the air and expelling Lenny. It lands upside down in the ditch, flames roaring. A few seconds later, the gas tank erupts into a fireball that lights up the night sky.

Tyler sees one of the bikers approaching. Just as he's about to warn Piper, Blade opens the driver's door and yanks Tyler out of the truck, sending him tumbling onto the road. He rolls to a stop, ending up face down and dazed but generally unharmed except for some road rash on his shoulder and forehead.

Piper swings sideways in her seat and kicks furiously at Blade as he tries to take control of the truck. As Blade struggles to overtake Piper, the truck slows. Tyler leaps up and runs alongside it. Piper sees a spray can rolling around on the floorboards, but she can't quite grab it. After a few more attempts, she finally succeeds. As Blade tries to subdue her kicking, she sprays him in the face with some degreaser, temporarily blinding him. At that moment, Tyler moves toward the tanker truck's cab bringing a hose with a heavy-duty nozzle on it. As Blade struggles to wipe the degreaser out of his eyes, Tyler hits Blade on the back of his head with the nozzle, and he falls out of the cab onto the road, unconscious. Wesley, who is following close behind, sees Blade fall and narrowly misses him as he lies motionless on the road. Tyler jumps back into the truck and hits the gas, so they can catch up to the Caddy.

Tyler glances over at Piper. "You OK?"

"I'm fine, but that poor biker isn't. How are you?"

"I'm OK. Just a few scratches. He got what he deserved."

Bernie looks over her shoulder and sees one of the bikers, Corry, pulling up on the convertible Caddy's passenger side. He grins at Bernie. Tony starts weaving from one side of the road to the other, making it difficult for Corry to attack them. Corry is wearing a perspiration-stained bandana and has a long, scruffy, bearded face with a scar over his right eye that bisects his eyebrow and continues down his cheek. He has a tall thin stature, and his torn T-shirt flaps in the wind as he leans over and pulls himself onto the Caddy's hood.

Bernie screams and grasps the pet carrier, causing Precious to start barking. Irene cowers in the rear seat, clutching her bags with her plants and seeds and tries to hide from view. Corry pulls himself across the hood, gripping the top of the windshield as he tries to reach over and force Tony to stop the car. Fearing for her life, Irene pulls the shotgun out from under the blanket next to her and points it at Corry, the barrel just over Tony's head. She closes her eyes and pulls the trigger. The shot misses Corry. Tony is shocked and deafened by the blast. He instinctively ducks to protect himself. Bernie searches frantically through her large handbag when she sees Corry attempt to punch Tony. She stops searching and feels down by her feet until she finds what she's been looking for. Just as Corry tries to pull himself up over the windshield to seize the steering wheel, Bernie tasers him in the face. As Tony swerves to the left, Corry slides over the hood and falls off the Caddy, ending up half on the road and half in the ditch.

"That was a close one!" Tony shouts. "Bernie, you did great!"

"I had to do something," Bernie replies. "He was trying to hurt us."

Tony looks back at Irene. "You nearly blew my head off! But I know you were just trying to help."

Irene looks up at Tony and just smiles at him.

Bernie looks down at Precious, and the dog looks up at her as if to say, "Thanks for protecting me."

With a big smile on her face, Irene leans forward and puts her hands on Tony and Bernie's shoulders while nodding to thank them for protecting her.

Boss Man and Hulk are rapidly approaching the lead truck with Boss Man on the driver's side and Hulk on the passenger side. Owen looks in his mirror and sees Boss Man approaching.

"We got company!" he screams. "Hold the shotgun so it's pointing out your window, and don't be afraid to use it!"

"I have one coming up fast on my side too," I exclaim. "I'm scared! I don't know if I can do this."

"We have to defend ourselves and protect the convoy," Owen insists. "Get ready."

At that moment, Boss Man jumps onto the step below the driver's door and points a handgun at Owen. "Stop the truck or I'll shoot!"

Owen grabs Boss Man's forearm and forces it up. It hits the top of the window opening. The gun discharges as Boss Man loses his grip, and the bullet smashes through the windshield in front of me. The gun drops to the floorboards. I panic and scream. At that moment, Hulk jumps onto my side of the truck next to the passenger door. I scream, close my eyes, and react by pulling the trigger on my shotgun. When I open my eyes, Hulk is nowhere to be seen.

Continuing to struggle with Boss Man, Owen lands a couple of solid punches, causing him to lose his grip and fall onto the road. He recovers quickly and climbs the rear ladder onto the top of the truck. He finds a short piece of pipe next to the roof rack and advances toward the front of the truck to attack Owen. Owen knows he's up there, so he starts climbing out of the cab.

"Kaylee, drive!"

"But I—"

"Just do it!"

I move over and grab the steering wheel. Then I nail the gas. The truck lurches forward, causing Boss Man to fall to his knees and Owen to swing sideways as he tries to climb on top of the truck.

Ronnie and Rosie watch as Owen faces off with Boss Man. Owen backs up as Boss Man swings the pipe. Owen manages to avoid being struck but is having difficulty defending himself. Seeing that he's in trouble, Rosie tells Ronnie to pull up closer to the lead truck. She climbs out of the cab and moves to the front of the truck. She clips the winch cable onto her belt and then jumps onto the rear ladder of the lead truck. She easily makes her way to the top of the truck, then forms a loop with the winch cable to snare Boss Man.

For some unknown reason, Boss Man turns his head and spots her out of the corner of his eye. Owen seizes the moment to knock the pipe out of the biker's hand, sending it falling onto the road. Then Owen punches Boss Man in the head. The biker stumbles back momentarily and then counter-attacks.

While dodging Boss Man's attacks, Owen manages to make the biker take a couple of steps back. Rosie springs forward and secures the winch cable around Boss Man's left ankle. She pulls the loop tight while moving rearward and jumps onto the front of the tanker truck while keeping tension on the cable. Then she turns on the winch, and it begins reeling in the cable. As the winch pulls up the slack, Boss Man tries desperately to free himself, but Owen attacks him and he has to defend himself. The cable tightens on Boss Man's ankle and pulls him back. He falls to his knees and struggles to prevent himself from sliding, to no avail. Owen watches as Boss Man topples from the lead truck and falls beside Rosie, hitting his head on the winch rendering him unconscious, his legs dragging on the pavement.

Owen returns to the cab, startling me as he pokes his slightly bloody face in the driver's window. "Kaylee, stop the truck!"

I slam on the brakes. Ronnie stops just short of hitting our truck sandwiching the unconscious biker's torso between our two vehicles. Rosie is holding onto the upper cross member of the bumper-mounted push bar while straddling the tanker's hood, having braced for impact.

The rest of the convoy catches up, and the group gathers to share their experiences and ponder Harley's absence. They immediately notice Boss Man hanging from the tanker's front bumper. Piper approaches Boss Man to see if he's conscious. He's not, but he's still breathing, so she tries to assess the severity of his injuries. Wesley suggests that he and Zac go back and see if they can find out what happened to Harley.

As they toss the first-aid kit into the back of their truck, they hear the sound of an approaching motorbike. Owen instructs everyone to hide behind the first two trucks as he runs to retrieve the rifle from his truck, and Wesley does likewise. As the motorbike approaches, they hear a clattering noise that sounds like the bike is dragging tin cans behind it. The mystery biker starts honking his horn, hopefully to deter Wesley and Owen from opening fire. Moments later, Harley pulls up in front of them with pots, pans, and kitchen utensils in tow.

Once the group comes out of hiding to greet Harley, he tells them that he dragged himself out of his burning truck and briefly lost consciousness. When he awakened, he salvaged what he could from his truck, hoping that he could catch up to the convoy. Fortunately, Harley only suffered a few scratches and non-severe burns and is generally OK. Everyone is relieved to know that Harley has survived.

Tony reports that they blew a front tire during the confrontation, so Wesley and Zac volunteer to install the spare. While the tire change is taking place, they remove Boss Man from the tanker truck's bumper and place him on a blanket in the ditch and bandage his wounds.

The convoy pushes on for a couple more hours and then pulls off the road to park as the sun rises to mark the beginning of another oppressively hot day. Some members of the group are worried that we could be attacked again, so Wesley appoints people to take turns keeping watch.

CHAPTER 27

The next evening as the sun sets, we depart on what should be our final night of travel if all goes well before we reach New Washington. After the first rest stop, one of the tanker trucks overheats, and we have to wait until the engine cools down to refill the cooling system with water. The moon brightens the night sky, and the stars provide a spectacular nocturnal vista. At 4:30 a.m., Owen and I see the silhouette of the New Washington domes in the distance. Travelling another hour brings us to an unpaved side road that ends at the food-production facility service entrance. Owen and I stop next to the loading ramp, and the rest of the convoy follows suit. Everyone gathers next to the loading ramp and forms a semicircle around Owen and me.

"OK, listen up, everyone," I say. "We have to stay together as a group, and we have to watch for security drones. They can appear at any time either outside or inside the building."

"Are we going with you, or should we wait here?" Tony asks.

"You have to come with us, or you might be spotted by a security drone," I reply.

"Follow us, and we'll find a place for you to wait," Owen says. "Kaylee and I will deal with Stanley and his plan to destroy VE—if we're not too late."

Wesley and Zac use a pry bar and hammer to loosen some of the roll-up door panels on one side without disturbing the security sensor contact. Owen and I enter first to make sure that the way is clear. Then the rest of the group enters the building, and we proceed single file along a dimly lit hallway with large pipes of varying colours on either side of us. The air is humid and has a musty smell as we periodically pass by access doors with fogged windows. I spot a drone up ahead and tell everyone to stand next to the wall as best as they can. The drone moves slowly toward us, stopping occasionally. The drone stops and looks directly at me for a few seconds and then moves on. Bernie receives the same treatment. Thankfully, Precious remains silent as everyone holds their breath. The drone continues on, and everyone breathes a sigh of relief.

I suggest that we enter the building proper to avoid the drones. We open the nearest access door and our group discovers that the building is a food-production facility housing livestock, fruit, and vegetables. The vertically suspended plants extend up toward the ceiling with light fixtures overhead that provide ultraviolet light. Water can be heard dripping from the automated irrigation system, but fortunately, no workers are to be seen. We proceed in single file down the narrow alleyways, sampling some of the fruit as we make our way to the front exit. I struggle to keep up with Owen as we go up the stairs and open the door slightly to see if anyone is around. We step out into the alleyway and note that there are no signs of life. We signal the rest of the group to join us and then cautiously approach the entrance to New Washington's central dome.

After passing through the opaque revolving door, Owen and I stop in our tracks and let out a gasp. The atmosphere in the dimly lit central dome has an eerie greenish tinge, and the air has a chemical odour unlike anything I've smelled before. Worse than that, thousands of dead bodies are heaped on one another. They're scattered everywhere, occupying all of the pathways in the promenade. The corpses have a powdery light-green hue and look like they would crumble if we touched them. Their grotesque facial expressions imply that the men, women, and children suffered terribly before they met their demise.

A few moments later, Owen and I return to prepare the group for what they are about to witness and explain that the inhabitants appear to have been subjected to a poisonous gas. With much trepidation, we carefully navigate our way around the bodies until we reach the Research Institute.

Prior to being evicted from New Washington, Stanley helped me create an alias security account and entry code so I could gain entry in the event that my code was blocked. I enter the alias code, and the green light on the keypad lights up as the lock releases. Keeping an eye out for security drones, I lead the group to the cafeteria and give my code to Wesley so everyone can have something to eat and drink. I instruct them to remain there while Owen and I depart to locate the Infinium computer system, which is housed beneath the Dream Palladium.

We traverse many narrow, concrete hallways that are more like tunnels. Soon we hear the sound of high-speed electric motors and approach the Infinium computer centre's service entrance. A yellow heavy-duty forklift is parked in a dedicated spot nearby. The doors are locked, and there are few other options in sight to gain entry. If we pry the doors open, the alarm will sound. Owen looks at the forklift.

"What are you thinking?" I ask.

"I'm going to punch a hole in the wall big enough for us to get through."

"The security drones might hear the noise," I caution.

Owen hops into the driver's seat and sees that the key is in the ignition. "It's a chance we'll have to take. Stand back."

Owen reverses the forklift a few feet. Then he roars forward and crashes into the thin concrete wall, creating an opening large enough to gain entry. He reverses the forklift and jumps off. Just then I spot a drone approaching.

"Owen, stand still and don't move," I warn.

We both remain motionless, expecting the alarm to sound at any moment. Instead, the drone makes a U-turn and, to our surprise, departs without noticing the hole in the wall.

As we enter the Infinium computer complex, the cooling fan noise is deafening, and we can feel an abundance of hot air blowing up from under the perforated floor as we navigate row after row of tall black monolithic towers with status panels containing rows of tiny blue pulsating LEDs. As we approach the far end of the complex, we see a massive master control panel and a communication console. A mesh access door next to the control panel is labelled "Authorized Personnel Only." I realize it must house the main circuit-breaker panel and padlocked master disconnect switch.

"What now?" Owen asks.

"I'm going to try to contact Stanley and talk him out of running his program."

I enter my alias username and password, allowing me to access the communications network. Entering a secret link connects me to Stanley's chat line.

"Stanley, can you hear me? It's your friend Kaylee. Hello. Are you there?"

There is no response for a few minutes, so I repeat my message. A few seconds later, I hear something, but the cooling fans make hearing difficult.

"Kaylee, is that you? What a nice surprise."

"Yes, it's me. Are you still at the off-site lab?"

"Yes. There are only two of us here now. Me and Earl."

"Why are you still there?"

"I stayed behind just in case there are any software glitches with VE to address."

"It must be lonely for you with no one to talk to."

"I don't need anyone to talk to," Stanley says. "Today is the day I've been waiting for. I'm going to take my revenge on the government and destroy VE. In fact, you can stay online if you want and I'll set you up with a video link so you can watch VE die too. It'll be fun."

"Stanley, you don't need to do this. Why don't you wait and think things over? Maybe the government can compensate you for your suffering."

"It's happening today, and that's final," Stanley insists.

I press the mute button on the console and glance over at Owen. "We need to be ready to flip the master power breaker."

"I can't," Owen replies. "It's locked in the 'on' position."

"Then you'll have to break the lock. Hurry!"

"There's a fire extinguisher and an axe in a glass case on the wall nearby. I'll use the axe to break the lock."

Repeated blows with the axe don't work, so Owen uses the tapered end of the axe to pry the lock free, damaging the breaker arm in the process.

"Well, here goes," Stanley says. "Die, VE, die."

"Now, Owen!" I scream. "Pull the breaker now!"

The damaged handle won't budge, so he strikes it with the axe and it trips the breaker. Alarm bells sound as the server towers lose power but only momentarily. The back-up battery power supply kicks in, and power is fully restored.

"What do we do now?" Owen yells. "The power's back on!"

"We'll have to sever the incoming fibre-optic communication feed. It's probably under the raised floor. Bring the axe, and we can try to find it. It will be a few minutes until the system returns to a fully operational status."

We open one of the hinged floor grates and slide on our stomachs into the cramped cavity, which is full of power-feed harnesses and fibre-optic cables. Moving about is difficult, and the air from the fans isn't helping. The open floor grate unexpectedly falls closed, concealing our whereabouts.

We hear footsteps close by and see two security guards standing overhead. We lay motionless, hoping they won't see us. We can barely hear over the fan noise as one of the guards gives an update to his supervisor over his communicator.

"We found a hole in the wall next to the computer centre door, but there's no sign of anyone in the computer centre, so whoever was in here must have left."

While searching for intruders, the security guards observe that the main power breaker has been deactivated. They receive permission to restore the power feed, causing the emergency lights and the alarm to turn off. We wait a few minutes to make sure the security guards have left and then resume our search for the fibre-optic communications feed.

"Owen, I think I can see the communications feed," I say. "Follow me."

Owen and I manage to circumnavigate many obstacles until we see an incoming feed label on the fibre-optic distribution box. A hinged floor grate directly above us is unwilling to cooperate as Owen struggles to open it. He strikes it a few times with the axe, and it finally pops open, though it falls back down on his arm. Though in pain, he props the grate open.

"Are you OK?" I ask.

"Yeah, I'll live. What now?"

"See those three large black cables coming from the grey steel box that's closest to the floor and is labelled 'Incoming Feed'? Those are the cables we need to cut."

Owen tries to sever them with the axe, but the insulation is seemingly impenetrable. After several futile attempts, he stops and tries to come up with plan B.

CHAPTER 28

Suddenly, Virtual Earth begins to shudder. A moment later, hundreds of people mysteriously vanish. Everyone struggles to maintain their balance, with some falling to the ground while tables and chairs topple over. Everyone in the promenade begins to panic, fearing for the worst.

Thomas is on the floor in his office when he calls Robert.

"Robert, what the hell is happening? It's as if VE is coming apart!"

"I think we're under attack," Robert replies. "Someone is trying to destroy VE using the Infinium computer system as the gateway to facilitate the attack., and I think it's an inside job."

"But who?" Thomas asks.

"I'll contact Earl Houseman to make sure that everyone has left the off-site base."

Robert switches to a comm that allows him to make contact with people outside of VE. "Earl, we have an emergency here in VE. We're under attack, and I think it's an inside job. Has everyone left the base?"

"Everyone except Stanley. He volunteered to remain on standby in case there are any VE software issues to address."

"I didn't ask Stanley to remain behind! You need to remove him from his computer terminal. If he refuses to cooperate, shoot him!"

"Will do," Earl replies. "Everyone in the lab knows he hates the government. He's been quite vocal on that topic to anyone who will listen."

Earl grabs a handgun from his desk, checks to ensure it's loaded, then hurries over to the lab, only to find the entry door blocked with furniture that Stanley manoeuvred into place with his power chair. Peeking through the two small windows in the door, Earl can't see Stanley, so he isn't able to shoot him.

"Robert, I can't get into the lab," Earl reports. "Stanley has blocked the door with furniture."

"Keep trying," Robert says. "We have to stop him!"

"OK," Earl replies.

"Thomas, one of the software programmers at the off-site base is responsible for the attack," Robert says. "Stanley Burke is his name. Earl Houseman is trying to stop him, but he can't gain access to the lab."

"Is there some other way we can stop Stanley from running his program?" Thomas asks.

"Yes. We have to prevent him from accessing the New Washington Infinium computer system. We've lost contact with security, though, so there's little chance short of a miracle that we'll be able to stop him from destroying VE."

CHAPTER 29

Owen notices a can of freezing spray used to cool down hot electronic components, likely left behind by one of the technicians. He sprays the cables until they're coated with a thick layer of frost. Because of his injured arm, he hands me the axe, and I strike the fibre-optic cables repeatedly, shattering them. The LEDs on the status panels of the monolithic server towers instantly go from a steady blue to flashing red. Alarms sound, and amber emergency lights activate around the perimeter of the computer centre.

"Kaylee, you did it!" Owen says. "You severed the cables!"

"Great! Now let's go and see if we've stopped Stanley from running his program," I say.

We hurry over to the communication console, where we find a message from Stanley.

"Kaylee, my program started to run and then stopped suddenly. Do you by chance know why?"

I hesitate for a moment and then respond.

"Yes, Stanley, I do. We stopped it, and you're in big trouble."

Stanley abruptly disconnects me from his link. Just then two security guards appear and confront us with their tasers primed and ready to use. Communications have been restored, and they inform Nikita Novikov, their supervisor, of our capture.

"We have them," one of the guards says. "They're in the computer centre. We've also detained a group of people we found in the Research Institute cafeteria. They said they were waiting for these two to return."

"Good work," Nikita says. "Bring all of them to the security office, and put the two you arrested in separate interrogation rooms."

When we reach the security office, Owen and I are separated and wait nervously to be questioned. The monitor mounted on the wall directly across from me turns on, and Nikita's face appears.

"You and your accomplice perpetrated an act of terrorism by purposely disabling the Infinium computer system in an attempt to shut Virtual Earth down," she says. "The result of such an act would have killed thousands of innocent people."

"But we—"

"Don't interrupt me! For this act you will be severely punished."

Just then Nikita receives a call from Thomas.

"Nikita, what's going on with the New Washington computer system? We had one of the memory pillars go offline. Everyone here is in a state of panic, and we need to know if further attacks on VE are imminent. What can you tell me?"

"We have arrested two individuals responsible for damaging the Infinium computer system," Nikita says.

"Who are they?"

"Kaylee Parker and Owen Kish."

"They're not criminals!" Thomas says. "They're heroes. They just saved over ninety percent of the population of VE! Let me speak to them."

Nikita escorts Owen to sit beside me. As Thomas's face appears on my monitor, we both fear the worst.

"Kaylee Parker, Owen Kish!" Thomas says. "I was just informed that you two purposely disabled the Infinium computer system. Is that true?"

"Yes, but we were—"

"Nikita stated that you two were arrested for performing an act of terrorism?"

"Yes, but we had to stop Stanley to save VE!" I reply. "Stanley was going to destroy everything!"

Thomas is silent for a few seconds. "I know why you disabled the Infinium computer, Kaylee. You and Owen are to be congratulated. If you two hadn't severed the Infinium computer communications link, VE surely would have been destroyed."

After a few seconds, Thomas continues, "I think in view of your heroic actions, you and your group deserve to be recognized." He conveys, "How would you and your friends like to come to VE? If you and your group agree, we can publicly thank you all for your outstanding bravery and perseverance that saved our world."

"Thank you," I reply. "When we learned of Stanley's evil plan, we had to do something. I'll discuss your invitation with the group."

Owen and I are soon reunited with the rest of our group in the security office cafeteria. Our friends are delighted to see us.

"Thank goodness you two are OK," Bernie says. "We heard alarms sounding and didn't know if we would ever see you again."

I grin at her. "Did you know we're being hailed as heroes?"

"For doing what?" Wesley asks. "All we did was wait for you two to return."

"For helping us get here, so we could stop Stanley from killing thousands of people," Owen says.

"And did we?" Piper asks.

"We managed to save over ninety percent of the population, so, yes, we were successful," I reply. "Thomas Williams, president of New Washington and New Los Angeles, has invited us to come to Virtual Earth to be recognized for our actions. Also, he's going to address the nation this evening."

The security guards prepare and distribute meals to the group. After supper, we gather around the monitor in the cafeteria, where Thomas appears.

"We experienced a near-fatal catastrophic event today that could have destroyed New Washington," Thomas says. "As a result of this act of terrorism, much damage was inflicted and many lives were lost. However, the impact of the incident was minimized thanks to a brave group of individuals. They travelled to New Washington and knowingly placed themselves in harm's way to stop this heinous act. I proclaim that tomorrow will be a national day of mourning where we will take time to remember those we lost and honour this heroic group of people who came to our rescue. Everyone is invited, and details of the ceremony will be announced soon. Be safe and goodnight."

After the presidential address, I ask everyone to remain for a brief meeting.

"Do we all agree to go to VE tomorrow for the ceremony?" I ask. "No one has to go, and you can all remain here if you wish. Please raise your hand if you want to go."

Everyone is in agreement with the invite. We decide to spend the night in the security office, using makeshift sleeping arrangements.

CHAPTER 30

The next morning, we're escorted through a series of underground passageways to the transfer hub located in the Research Institute's high-security underground vault. Nikita informs us that after we migrate to Virtual Earth, we will have to go through an immigration process wherein we will be registered as temporary residents. Everyone except me is fitted with a temporary uplink port and then given an injection of intelligent nano-probes.

Upon arrival at the transfer hub, we're assigned individual chambers, including Precious. We place our belongings on a shelf next to our reclining chairs, which are fitted with clear canopies and are in the raised upright position. Once seated, the lights dim, and the canopies lower, covering our heads and upper bodies. Precious is fitted with a special temporary uplink port along with an injection of nano-probes and put in a bin with a clear top that has a happy gas supply tube connected to it. We all receive a small dose of happy gas to put us to sleep.

When we awaken, our chamber lights switch on, and we gather any loose belongings placed on the shelf prior to departure. The chamber doors slide open, and we gather together, commenting to one another that we feel great and don't sense that anything has physically changed. With a sneer on my face, I'm not impressed, but I admit that my legs function much better there.

"That was a quick trip," Tony says. "It doesn't feel like we've gone anywhere."

"That's because your body didn't go anywhere," I explain. "The only difference is your mind is no longer in the real world, although you wouldn't know it."

A tall, slender young lady dressed in a light-blue security uniform leads us up a set of stairs to the main floor of the building. Two administration desks are at the front of a roped-off area where everyone lines up to be processed. The front wall facing the promenade is all glass with an emergency exit at the far end. As we look out the windows, we see people sitting at nearby cafés and others strolling along the promenade walkways. It has been declared a holiday, so much of the population is there, making it somewhat crowded.

After processing, we're escorted through the promenade to the Dream Palladium, where a temporary stage has been set up out front. Once inside the Dream Palladium, we're offered refreshments and briefed on the festivities that are to take place in the afternoon. Everyone is quite impressed with what they see in a world they never could have envisioned a few days ago.

At 1:50 p.m., we're escorted to a seating area at the back of the temporary stage where we can look out over the promenade and enjoy our new environment.

At 2:00 p.m., Thomas and other dignitaries walk onto the stage. They are greeted with enthusiastic rounds of applause and cheers from the huge crowd as trumpets play ceremonial introductory music similar to the Romans announcing the arrival of their emperor. The crowd settles, and Thomas walks over to the lectern at the front of the stage.

"Certain events took place yesterday that defy explanation. People suddenly disappeared, and part of our city is a white haze behind an impenetrable transparent wall. What I have to tell you next will be very disturbing, and I know that many of you'll be in a state of shock. To preserve our world from certain disaster, we were recently forced to migrate to a place called Virtual Earth."

The crowd is extremely upset and responds with jeers and boos. It's several minutes before Thomas can continue.

"We were forced to do so on very short notice because rebels attacked our oxygen-enhancement facility, resulting in our air supply being poisoned. New Los Angeles was attacked as well, but their oxygen-enhancement facility was not damaged. I'm sorry for springing this upon you so suddenly, but it can't be helped. I can tell you that occupying Virtual Earth is deemed temporary, and we have a plan in place to return to the real world eventually. I'll hold a televised question-and-answer forum in the near future to further explain our situation."

Thomas steps aside to allow the crowd to settle down.

"The ceremony will continue following a short intermission," an announcer says.

The audience is still somewhat unsettled as Thomas returns to the stage a few minutes later.

"We're gathered here today to remember those citizens lost as a result of an unspeakable act of terrorism. Our hearts go out to their families and friends as we all grieve the loss of so many souls. As an expression of respect, we will now have two minutes of silence to remember and reflect upon what has just transpired."

Everyone is silent with their heads bowed until trumpets signal the end of the time of remembrance. Everyone remains silent until Thomas continues the ceremony.

"At this time, it is my privilege to introduce you to a special group of people who, at great risk to themselves, persevered to come to our aid. These people have no direct linkage to our world but still went above and beyond to avert a catastrophe."

Thomas motions us to come forward and line up behind him as he turns to face us.

"We have Owen Kish, Kaylee Parker, Tony Bianchi, Bernice Bianchi, Irene Ho, Tyler Wagner, Piper Wagner, Ronnie Wagner, Rosie Wagner, Wesley Steils, Zac LaFrosche, and Harley Clemson. Oh, I almost forgot. We also have Bernie's dog, Precious."

The crowd offers generous applause and cheers that continue for some time. Thomas summons Owen and I to come forward and stand beside him.

"These two individuals deserve special recognition," he says. "Upon learning of the terrorist plot to destroy us, Kaylee and Owen unselfishly took the initiative to travel to New Washington. While putting themselves in great danger, they stopped the terrorist from completing his mission. As a token of our appreciation, I would like to invite Owen and Kaylee and every member of their group to take up residence here in New Washington, if they so wish. We'll forever be indebted to them for their selfless act of bravery that saved our city."

The audience cheers and whistles once again. When the ceremony concludes, the inside surface of the dome is ablaze with a dazzling display of virtual fireworks set to music. Afterward, the audience reflects upon what has just transpired with some people continuing with a subdued celebration well into the night.

We're ushered back into the Dream Palladium, where we discuss our options.

"Tony, just think," Bernie says. "We can live here and have a comfortable life."

"Yup, that would suit me. Then I wouldn't have to worry about you if something happened to me," Tony replies.

"Best offer I've heard all day," Harley says. "I'm stayin'."

"We are too," Tyler says.

Irene nods in agreement.

"We're lucky that Kaylee and Owen came along when they did," Wesley says. "I'm not so sure we would have survived otherwise."

"You two guys are the greatest!" Zac says. "And I'm not going anywhere. I like it here."

We are assigned temporary lodging and disperse to join in with the festivities. Owen and I explore the promenade and eventually find a quiet corner at one of the busy sidewalk cafés.

"I didn't hear you say that you wanted to stay here," Owen says.

"No, you didn't. I finally fixed my spinal cord, and I want to live in the real world so I can use my real legs and not be some sort of digital freak."

"Whoa, that's harsh."

"You'd feel the same if you'd been stuck in a wheelchair for most of your life," I insist.

"Fair enough," Owen replies, nodding. "I don't think we're being held captive. Thomas said we can choose to stay or leave."

"You and I know that we can't leave. All they have to do is dispose of our real bodies, leaving us with no other option than to stay."

Owen falls silent. He clearly hadn't thought of that.

CHAPTER 31

Later that night, while most of the city is asleep, I pack my meagre belongings along with the toiletry kit they gave us and quietly disappear out of the building. I crouch low and stay close to the elevated flowerbeds to avoid being detected by security drones. Seeing one in the distance, I watch as it continues on, not noticing me.

As I approach the Research Institute's side entrance, another drone appears out of nowhere and spots me. I see two security guards heading in my direction as I enter my alias passcode into the illuminated keypad next to the entrance, hoping it will work, which it does. The lock releases and I gain entry, then force the door to close just before the security guards arrive. They are denied access, as they do not have permission to enter the highly secure Research Institute labs. They pound on the door in frustration as I glance back at them while heading for the transfer hub. It will take them some time to figure out my real identity.

I hurry through the darkened hallways to the transfer hub. As I prepare to depart, I am tempted to bring a solar-charging communicator along so I can stay in touch with

Owen. But I suddenly realize that they only exist inside of VE.

After disabling the transfer hub door's keypad and jamming the door with a chair, I use the same cubicle that I occupied previously. I can hear the security guards tugging at the door as I transfer back to the real New Washington hub.

When I awaken, I put on my oxy-pack and then exit the Research Institute, noticing immediately that the air is stale and lacking oxygen. My legs hurt, and I'm once again appalled at the sight of thousands of corpses littering the promenade. I attempt to crouch and maintain a low profile, watching for security guards and drones as I navigate my way to the food-production facility.

A drone unexpectedly makes an appearance and notifies a pair of security personnel of my whereabouts. They immediately inform Nikita that they are in pursuit and move toward me while manoeuvring around numerous corpses. I nearly trip as my foot kicks a corpse's arm, causing the powdery flesh to fall off and exposing the skeletal arm and hand bones. Upon seeing the bones, I gasp. Then I struggle to pull myself up, knowing there is no time to spare to reach the food-production facility entrance.

When I reach the food-production facility, I have some difficulty with the steps leading down to the entrance. Once inside, the air quality is noticeably better, and I can breathe without my oxy-pack. I know the layout of the facility from when Jess and I volunteered to help with the setup, and I make my way expediently through the narrow vegetation-lined alleyways, the plants helping to conceal me. Stopping for a moment to catch my breath, I gather some fruit and vegetables into a discarded apron to take with me to enjoy at my new home.

Having reached the livestock pens, I decide to let the chickens, turkeys, and rabbits out of their cages to slow the security guards down. Feathers fly as the birds and animals escape and block the alleyways. Then I make for the roll-up maintenance door we used previously so I can make my escape.

Upon reaching the livestock section, the security guards' efforts to get through are thwarted by hundreds of chickens, turkeys, and rabbits. They backtrack out of the livestock compound and find an alternate route.

Hurrying down the outer hallway, I see the roll-up door on the left, sixty feet ahead. Though my legs are aching, I push on as if I'm in a race and nearing the finish line.

Just as I approach the roll-up door, the security guards race out into the hallway, blocking my way. Both guards draw their tasers and aim them at me. Fearing the worst, I'm so scared that I'm shaking while protecting my face with my arms and feeling like I might faint.

One of the security guards informs Nikita that they have me trapped in the food-production facility and are preparing to subdue me if I resist. However, Thomas has contacted Nikita and informed Nikita that I do not pose any threat to security and am free to leave New Washington if I so choose. Nikita contacts the security guards and informs them to stand down.

The security guards suddenly stop, switch off their tasers, and holster them.

I lower my arms and stare at them in confusion. "Am I not under arrest?"

"We've been instructed to release you and let you leave New Washington, if that is your wish," a guard says.

"Yes. That is my wish, and I'm leaving now," I reply.

Once outside, I load supplies from the other vehicles into the lead truck. Some of the chickens are nearby, so I coax them back into their enclosure in the lead truck. Then I refuel and head over to Flatlands National Park. I visited the park while on vacation many years ago. It's about a two-hour drive from New Washington.

Upon my arrival, I fill my backpack with fruit and vegetables and some non-perishable food items along with flasks of water and bring a rifle. I hesitate for a moment, wondering if I have made a wise decision separating myself from Owen. Then I reassure myself that this is what I want to do.

"Hang in there, chickens," I mumble. "I'll be back tomorrow to get you."

I follow the path next to a rock face on my right and a sheer cliff on my left that descends to the valley floor, knowing it will eventually take me to the visitors' centre. Gaining elevation quickly, I experience some challenges with fallen rock impeding my progress. As I move to a higher elevation, at one point, the path has been severely damaged by falling rock and is just wide enough to allow passage. Not being fond of heights, I proceed cautiously, my nose almost touching the rock face as I try not to look down at the valley floor 200 feet below.

When I reach the visitors' centre, it appears to be fairly intact. The windows and doors are covered in fine dust and were sandblasted when the firestorm passed by, so I can't see inside. A large sand drift blocks access to the centre, so I scoop away enough sand with my foot to allow me to open one of the doors. I expected them to be locked, but to my amazement, they're not. Everyone must have left in a hurry. At first glance, it appears to be undisturbed with heavy layers of dust on every horizontal surface, including the floor. I call out to ask if anyone is there and hear only the echo of my own voice. Then I walk over to the snack shop on the far side of the centre, wipe the dust from the counter, and set my backpack down.

I dust off a chair, sit, and nibble on some grapes that I procured from the food-production facility. After resting for a while, I observe a small chameleon high up on the wall behind the food-service counter.

"Well, I guess it's just you and me living here from now on," I say.

CHAPTER 32

A first-aid room sign with an arrow pointing to the left brings me to a small room where there is a cabinet filled with first-aid supplies and a small sink on one side as well as a dusty cot with a pillow on the other side of the room. I lift the blanket to remove some of the dust and then sit on the cot. The dust makes me sneeze. I notice that one of the drawers on the cabinet reads "Snake Bite Kit," which reminds me of a rattlesnake that I once saw sleeping on a rock.

Back in New Washington, Owen awakens in the morning and knocks on my door, with no response. He knocks again with the same result. He presses the "open" button on the keypad, and to his surprise, the door opens. Upon entering, he finds an empty bed and my belongings missing.

"She didn't," Owen mutters.

He notices a crudely drawn map on a pillowcase with directions to Flatlands National Park and is marked with an "X" indicating her destination.

Owen leaves the building in search of the security office. He arrives just in time to greet Nikita as she arrives.

"Nikita, good morning. I need to talk to you," Owen says.

"It's about Kaylee, isn't it?" she says. "Do you know she left New Washington?"

"I suspected she did because her stuff is missing from her room," Owen confides.

Nikita nods. "That's correct. Once we were notified that she was not a threat to security, we didn't try to stop her from leaving. You can go as well, if you so desire."

"Yes, I definitely want to go and be with Kaylee as soon as possible."

After he gathers his personal items, he is taken to the transfer hub and upon returning to the real world is escorted by security to the food-production facility exit where their vehicles are parked. He sees that the lead truck is gone, so he gasses up the last truck using fuel from a nearby service truck and then briefly studies the map drawn on the pillow case before departing.

Travel is uneventful other than dodging sand drifts on the park access road. He can see evidence of another vehicle having used the road recently.

Upon reaching the visitors' parking lot, he spots Kaylee's truck. As he parks beside it, he hears chickens cackling in the back. After verifying that their oxygen supplement equipment is functioning, he tosses a handful of feed into their enclosure. He sees Kaylee's footprints in the sand drifts that are scattered along the pathway as he makes his way to the visitors' centre.

Somewhat frightened when I hear noises, I take my rifle and hide behind the ticket kiosk next to the entrance doors. When I hear the door open, I jump out.

"Stop or I'll shoot!"

"Whoa. Don't shoot! It's me, Owen," he says, his hands raised.

I lower my rifle and set it down next to the kiosk. Then I step out from behind the kiosk and hug him. Owen pulls back and looks me in the eyes. Then we both lean in for a kiss.

"I'm so glad you came," I say. "I wasn't sure if you would want to come or not, and I thought they might not let you leave New Washington."

Having released me, Owen puts his arms around me again and pulls me close. "No. Surprisingly, I talked to Nikita, and they let me leave to be with you. I just had to come and be with you. There's no other place I'd rather be."

After supper, Owen and I explore various walkways and natural elements, such as fossils that are on display embedded in the rock walls. We notice a narrow vertical opening at the back of the centre with air blowing in from an unknown source. The air is cool and seems to be oxygen enriched, as our breathing is quite normal without the need to wear our oxy-packs.

Farther down a curved, cave-like hallway we find an unmarked steel door with a rack beside it on which are a series of colour-coded research binders on plant growth.

Upon opening the door, we see a narrow path with steep rock walls on either side. Above is a cloudless sky. Curiosity getting the better of us, we test the air quality and find it to be OK. Following the winding path, we see that it opens up on our left to reveal a long, narrow rock-walled canyon with a shallow river flowing through it and bordered on both sides by lush greenery with many tropical trees and plants. To our right is the entrance to a large cavern-like rock structure.

After taking in the breathtaking beauty of the natural elements that surrounds us, we walk onto a sandy beach. Looking into the large river-fed pool originating from a spring far back in the cavern, we watch minnows swimming in crystal-clear water, looking for food. A few birds fly by and disappear as we traverse the canyon. The air is pleasantly warm and seems to be OK to breathe as there is an outflow of air from the cavern that could possibly be oxygen enriched.

Having high rock walls on either side of the river means that the exposure of the riverbanks to the sun is limited, and the environment is ideal for plant life to flourish. On the far side of the river, sand had been deposited below the rock face along with some fallen rock, and we assume it resulted from when the firestorm came through. Even with all of the sand that has accumulated there, some plants have managed to grow. Owen dips his hand in the water and takes a sip. He tells me that the water tastes great, likely due to the river being spring fed. We head back up to the visitors' centre to prepare our sleeping arrangements.

Owen looks at me and glances at the cot in the first-aid room, but I shake my head, indicating that we are *not* sharing it. Owen accepts my terms and gathers some cushions from the couches in the lounge, setting his bed up in the hallway next to the first-aid room.

Before turning in, we sit out on the viewing platform overlooking the valley floor far below the visitors' centre. Despite the windows being somewhat opaque, we can see red rocks of varying sizes and shapes poking out of the sand and a ridge of jagged red rock along the horizon. The evening is very peaceful as we watch the sun go down on our first night together in our new home.

As daylight fades into darkness, we close the door to the centre and then turn in for the night. It has been a long, trying day for both of us. We end our day with a kiss and then settle in for a good night's sleep.

The next morning, we return to the trucks to retrieve some more supplies, including the remaining food and some plants and ponder what to do with the chickens that somehow managed to survive with little to no food or water.

Slightly puzzled, Owen notices a plume of dust in the distance where the park road meets the highway, implying that one or more vehicles are approaching. With our rifles in hand, he and I watch as the Caddy and then the water tanker truck come into view. After they round the last curve before entering the parking lot, they soon pull up next to Owen and I, who are standing there in disbelief. In the Caddy are Tony, Bernie, Precious, and Irene with Tyler and Piper in the water tanker's cab and Ronnie and Rosie riding on top.

"What are you guys doing here?" I ask, dumbfounded. "Are you crazy? You didn't have to come on my account."

"We're family, so we thought we should all stick together," Bernie says.

"What about Wesley, Zac, and Harley?" Owen asks.

"They decided to stay in Virtual New Washington so they can settle down and begin a new adventure."

"So, where are you two staying?" Piper inquires.

"We've moved into the visitors' centre," I reply. "Bring what you can, and we'll take you there, but be warned, the path is somewhat challenging in places."

As we proceed up the path, some members of the group are nervous as they inch along the short stretch of narrow rock ledge where the path is damaged. Once we arrive at the visitors' centre, however, they are delighted with their surroundings and not having to wear their oxy-packs while inside.

We all have lunch together on the glass-enclosed balcony overlooking the valley and then rest for a while. Later in the afternoon, everyone gathers together in the lounge.

Bernie summons Owen and me to stand next to her. "Kaylee and Owen, we have a housewarming gift for you," she says.

Tony disappears briefly and returns with a thin, rectangular object wrapped in a beach towel. Owen and I take it from Tony and open it. It's the sign from the campground they called home, and it's updated to read: "The New Little Eden RV and Trailer Park. All Are Welcome."

With a tear forming in the corner of my eye, I thank everyone for joining us, as does Owen. He asks the group to follow him to the visitors' centre entrance. He places the sign on a rock ledge just outside the door for all to see.

I announce that Owen and I have a surprise for them too and take them for a tour of the canyon. Irene is so excited to see that she will have a place for her garden and chickens. The others are delighted that everything is going to work out well in our new home. There's a small town not far from the park, and I suggest that Ronnie and Rosie go there soon and see what they can salvage to make our accommodations more comfortable.

Later that evening, when everyone is sleeping, Owen and I sit out on the visitors' balcony enjoying the serenity of our new home.

"It's been quite a day, hasn't it?" Owen says.

I feel incredibly comfortable cuddling next to him. I look up at him and smile.

"Yes, it has. We're all together now, and everything is perfect. It's like we're living in a dream."

Printed in Canada